A DAUGHTER OF THE VINE

Owing to the antiquity and rarity of this book, certain pages are regrettably absent, and readability is compromised due to the blurring of the original text. If you possess any insights regarding the availability of these missing sections, kindly inform us. Your assistance is crucial in ensuring the completion of this significant work for the benefit of future generations.

A DAUGHTER OF THE VINE

GERTRUDE ATHERTON

GYAN

Published by

Gyan Publishing House
5, Ansari Road
Daryaganj, New Delhi-110002
Phone: 011-47034999, 9811692060
E-mail: books@gyanbooks.com

Distribution Network
gyanbooks.com
India, USA, Canada, UK, Australia

ISBN: 978-93-6780-262-5 (HB)
First Published, 1923

2nd Impression 2024

Printed at: Gyan Press, Delhi.

A DAUGHTER OF THE VINE
Author: GERTRUDE ATHERTON

A DAUGHTER OF THE VINE

A DAUGHTER OF THE VINE

BY

GERTRUDE ATHERTON

Author of
"Senator North," "The Californians," etc.

NEW YORK
DODD, MEAD AND COMPANY
1923

BOOK I

A Daughter of the Vine

BOOK I

I

Two horses were laboriously pulling a carriage through the dense thickets and over the sandhills which in the early Sixties still made an ugly breach between San Francisco and its Presidio. The difficulties of the course were not abridged by the temper of the night, which was torn with wind and muffled in black. During the rare moments when the flying clouds above opened raggedly to discharge a shaft of silver a broad and dreary expanse leapt into form. Hills of sand, bare and shifting, huge boulders, tangles of scrub oak and chaparral, were the distorted features of the landscape between the high far-away peaks of the city and the military posts on the water's edge. On the other side of the bay cliffs and mountains jutted, a mere suggestion of outline. The ocean beyond the Golden Gate roared over the bar. The wind whistled and shrilled through the rigging of the craft on the bay; occasionally it lifted a loose drift and whirled it about the carriage, creating a little cyclone with two angry eyes, and wrenching loud curses from the man on the box.

"It's an unusually bad night, Thorpe, really," said one of the two occupants of the carriage. "Of course the winters here are more or less stormy, but we have many fine days, I assure you; and they're better than the summer with its fogs and trade winds — I am speaking of San Francisco," he added hastily, with newly acquired Californian pride. "Of course it is usually fine in the country at any time. I believe there are sixteen different climates in California."

"As any one of them might be better than England's, it is not for me to complain," said the other, good-naturedly. "But I feel sorry for the horses and the man. I don't think we should have missed much if we had cut this ball."

"Oh, I would n't miss it for the world. Life would be suicidal in this God-forsaken country if it were not for the hospitality of the San Franciscans. Some months ago two officers whose names I won't mention met in a lonely spot on the coast near Benicia Fort, on the other side of the bay, with the deliberate intention of shooting one another to death. They were discovered in time, and have since been transferred East. It is better for us on account of San Francisco — Whew! how this confounded thing does jolt! — and the Randolph parties are always the gayest of the season. Mr. Randolph is an Englishman with the uncalculating hospitality of the Californian. He has made a pot of money and entertains lavishly. Every pretty girl in San Francisco is a belle, but Nina Randolph is the belle *par excellence.*"

"Is she a great beauty?" asked Thorpe, indifferently. He was wondering if the driver had lost his way. The wheels were zigzagging through drifts so deep that the sand shot against the panes.

"No, I don't know that she is beautiful at all. Miss Hathaway is that, and Mrs.

McLane, and two of the 'three Macs.' But she has it all her own way. It's charm, I suppose, and then — well, she's an only child and will come in for a fortune — a right big one if this place grows as people predict. She's a deuced lucky girl, is Miss Nina Randolph, and it will be a deuced lucky fellow that gets her. Only no one does. She's twenty-three and heart-whole."

"Are you in love with her?"

"I'm in love with her and Guadalupe Hathaway and the 'three Macs' and Mrs. McLane. I never met so many attractive women in one place."

"Would it be Mrs. Hunt McLane — a Creole? I met her once in Paris—got to know her very well."

"You don't say. She'll make things hum for you. There's something else I wanted to say. I thought I'd wait and see if you discovered it yourself, but I believe I won't. It's this: there's something queer about the Randolphs in spite of the fact that they're more to the front than any people in San Francisco. I never leave that house that I don't carry away a vague impression that there 's something behind the scenes I don't know anything about. I 've never spoken of it to anyone else; it would be rather disloyal, after all the kindness they 've shown me; but I 'm too curious to know how they will impress you. I 've only been here six months, and only know what everybody else knows about them —"

"Do you know, Hastings," said the Englishman abruptly, "I think something is wrong outside. I don't believe anyone is guiding those horses."

Hastings lowered the window beside him and thrust out his head.

"Hi, there, Tim!" he shouted. "What are you about?"

There was no reply.

"Hello!" he cried, thinking the wind might have miscarried his voice.

Again there was no reply; but the horses, gratefully construing the final syllable to their own needs, came to a full stop.

Hastings opened the door and sprang on to the hub of the wheel, expostulating angrily. He returned in a moment to his companion.

"Here's the devil to pay," he cried. "Tim 's down against the dashboard as drunk as a lord. There 's nothing to do but put him inside and drive, myself. I 'd chuck him into a drift if I were not under certain obligations of a similar sort. Will you come outside with me, or stay in with him?"

"Why not go back to the Presidio?"

"We are about half-way between, and may as well go on."

"I 'll go outside, by all means."

He stepped out. The two men dragged the coachman off the box and huddled him inside.

"We 're off the road," said Hastings, "but I think I can find my way. I 'll cut across to the Mission road, and then we 'll be on level ground, at least."

They mounted the box. Hastings gathered the reins and Thorpe lit a cigar. The horses, well ordered brutes of the livery stable, did their weary best to respond to the peremptory order to speed.

"We 'll be two hours late," the young officer grumbled, as they floundered out of the sandhills and entered the Mission Valley.

"Damn the idiot. Why could n't he have waited till we got there?"

They were now somewhat sheltered from the wind, and as the road was level, although rutty, made fair progress.

"I did n't mean to treat you to a nasty adventure the very night of your arrival," continued Hastings apologetically.

"Oh, one rather looks for adventures in California. If I had'n t so much sand in my eyes I 'd be rather entertained than otherwise. I only hope our faces are not dirty."

"They probably are. Still, if we are not held up, I suppose we can afford to overlook the minor ills."

"Held up?"

"Stopped by road-agents, garroters, highway robbers — whatever you like to call 'em. I 've never been held up myself; as a rule I go in the ambulance at night, but it 's no uncommon experience. I 've got a revolver in my overcoat pocket — on this side. Reach over and get it, and keep it cocked. I *could n't* throw up my hands. I 'd feel as if the whole United States army were disgraced."

Thorpe abstracted the pistol, but although

the long lonely road was favourable to crime, no road-agents appeared, and Hastings drove into the outskirts of the town with audibly expressed relief.

"We 're not far now," he added. "South Park is the place we 're bound for; and, by the way, Mr. Randolph projected and owns most of it."

A quarter of an hour later he drove into an oval enclosure trimmed with tall dark houses, so sombre in appearance that to the old Californian they must now, in their desertion and decay, seem to have been grimly prescient of their destiny.

As the carriage drew up before a brilliantly lighted house the door opened, and a manservant ran down the steps.

"Keep quiet," whispered Hastings.

The man opened the door of the carriage, waited a moment, then put his head inside. He drew it back with a violent oath.

"It 's a damned insult!" he cried furiously.

"Why, Cochrane!" exclaimed Hastings, "what on earth is the matter with you?"

"Captain Hastings!" stammered the man. "Oh I — I — beg pardon. I thought —

Oh, of course, I see. Tim had taken a drop too much. A most deplorable habit. Can I help you down, sir?"

"No, thanks."

He sprang lightly to the sidewalk, followed with less agility by the Englishman, who still held the cocked pistol.

"I forgot about this thing," said Thorpe. "Here — take it. I suppose we don't enter the houses of peaceable citizens, even in California, carrying loaded firearms?"

Cochrane led the horses into the little park which prinked the centre of the enclosure, and the young men ascended the steps.

"I'd give a good deal to know what set him off like that," said Hastings. "Hitherto he's been the one thoroughly impassive creature I've met in California; has a face about as expressionless as a sentinel on duty."

He pushed open the door and they entered a large hall lavishly decorated with flowers and flags. Many people were dancing in a room at the right, others were strolling about the hall or seated on the stair. These made way rather ungraciously for the late comers, who went hurriedly up to the dressing-room and regarded themselves in the mirror.

"We're not dirty, after all," said the Englishman in a tone of profound relief. He was a tall thin man of thirty or less with a dark face lean enough to show hard ungraceful lines of chin and jaw. The mouth would have been sensual had it been less determined, the grey eyes cold had they been less responsive to humour. Mrs. McLane had told him once that he was the type of man for whom civilization had done most: that an educated will and humour, combined with high breeding, had saved him from slavery to the primal impulses. His voice was harsh in tone but well modulated. He held himself very erectly but without self-consciousness.

Hastings' legs were his pride, and there were those who averred that they were the pride of the Presidio. His face was fair and round, his eyes were as talkative as his tongue. A past master of the noble art of flirting, no one took him more seriously than he took himself. He spoke with the soft rich brogue of the South; to-day it is hardened by years of command, and his legs are larger, but he is a doughty general, eager as ever for the hot high pulse of battle.

"Come on, Dud," he said, "time is getting short."

As they walked down the stair a man who was crossing the hall looked up, smiled charmingly, then paused, awaiting them. He was a small man of dignified presence with a head and face nobly modelled. His skin was faded and worn, it was cut with three or four deep lines, and his hair was turning grey, but his black eyes were brilliant.

"Don't turn us out, Mr. Randolph," cried Hastings. "It was not indifference that made us late; it was an ill-timed combination of Tim and rum. This is the English friend you were kind enough to say I could bring," he added as he reached the hall. "Did I tell you his name?—Thorpe, Dudley Thorpe, of Hampshire. That may interest you. You English are almost as sectional as we are."

Mr. Randolph had already grasped Thorpe's hand warmly and was bidding him welcome. "My home was further north—Yorkshire," he said. "Come into the parlour and meet my wife and daughter." As they pushed their way through the crowd he "sized up" the stranger with the rapid scrutiny of that period. "You must make yourself at home in my house," he said abruptly. "There are few English here and I am more glad than I can express to meet you."

"Ah — thanks!" Thorpe was somewhat taken aback, then remembered that he was in the newest section of the new world. And he had heard of the hospitality of the Californian.

They had entered a large room, canvassed for the evening and denuded of all furniture except the long rows of chairs against the walls. The musicians were resting. Men were fanning girls flushed and panting after the arduous labours of the waltz of that day. At one end of the room were some twenty or thirty older women.

Thorpe looked about him curiously. The women were refined and elegant, many of them with beauty or its approximate; three or four were Spanish, black-eyed, magnetic with coquetry and grace. The men, even the younger men, had a certain alertness of expression, a cool watchful glance; and they were all gentlemen. This fact impressed Thorpe at once, and as they walked down the long room something he said betrayed his thoughts.

"Yes," said Mr. Randolph, quickly. "They are all from the upper walks of life—men who thought there would be a better chance for them in the new community than in even the older American ones. And they keep together because, naturally, they are the law-abiding class and responsible for the future of the country. That also accounts for what you find in their faces. This sort of life develops character very quickly. There is another element in California. You will see it—Ah! here is my wife."

A tall raw-boned woman with weak blue eyes and abundant softly piled hair had arisen from the group of matrons and was advancing toward them. She was handsomely dressed in black velvet, her neck covered with point lace confined under the loose chin by a collar of diamonds.

She looked cold and listless, but spoke pleasantly to the young men.

"We are glad to welcome an Englishman,"

she said to Thorpe; and to Hastings: "You are not usually so late, and I have heard a round dozen inquiring for you."

Thorpe, as he exchanged commonplaces with her, reflected that no woman had ever attracted him less. As he looked into the face he saw that it was cold, evil, and would have appeared coarse but for the hair and quiet elegance of attire. Despite her careful articulation, he detected the broad *o* and *a* of the Yorkshire people. The woman was playing the part of a gentlewoman and playing it fairly well. When the thin lips moved apart in an infrequent smile they displayed sharp scattered teeth. The jaw was aggressive. The hands in their well-adjusted gloves were large even for her unusual height. As Thorpe remarked that he was prepared to admire and enjoy California, one side of her upper lip lifted in an ugly sneer.

"Probably," she replied coldly. "Most people catch it. It's like the measles. I wish Jim Randolph liked it less."

Thorpe, for the first time, experienced a desire to meet Nina Randolph.

Hastings disengaged him. "Come," he

said, "I'll introduce you to Miss Randolph and one or two others, and then you can look out for yourself. I want to dance. Mrs. McLane is not here. There are the 'three Macs,'" indicating a trio surrounded by a group of men, — "Miss McDermott, classic and cold; Miss McAllister, languid and slight; Miss McCullum, stocky and matter-of-fact. But it will take you a week to straighten them out. Here — look — what do you think of this?"

Thorpe directed his glance over the shoulders of a knot of men who surrounded a tall Spanish-looking girl with large haughty blue eyes and brown hair untidily arranged. She wore an old black silk frock with muslin bertha. Her face interested Thorpe at once, but in a moment he had much ado to keep from laughing outright. For she spoke never a word. She merely *looked*; taking each eager admirer in turn, and by some mysterious manipulation of eyelash, sweeping a different expression into those profound obedient orbs every time. As she saw Hastings she nodded carelessly, and, when he presented Thorpe, spoke for the first time.

She merely said "Good-evening," but her voice, Spanish, low, sweet — accompanied by a look — made the stranger feel what a blessed thing hospitality was.

"So that is your Miss Hathaway," he said, as Hastings once more led him onward. "What a pity that such a beautiful girl should be so poor. But she 'll probably marry any one of these incipient millionaires she wants."

"Poor?" cried Hastings. "Oh, her get-up. She affects to despise dress — or does. God forbid that I should presume to understand what goes on behind those blue masks. Her father is a wealthy and distinguished citizen. Her mother inherited a hundred thousand acres from one of the old grandees. What do you think of her?"

"Her methods are original and entertaining, to say the least. Does she never — converse?"

"When she has something to say; she 's a remarkable woman. That must be Miss Randolph. Her crowd is always the densest."

As Thorpe was presented to Nina Randolph he forgot that he was a student of heredity. He had never seen so radiant and triumphant a being. She seemed to him, in that first moment, to symbolize the hope and joy and individualism of the New World. Small, like her father, she was perfectly modelled, from her round pulsing throat to the tips of her tiny feet: ignoring the fashion, her yellow gown fitted her figure instead of a hoop-skirt. Her black hair was coiled low on her head, but, although unconfined in a net, did not, like Miss Hathaway's "waterfall," suggest having been arranged in the dark. Her black eyes, well set and wide apart, sparkled with mirth. The head was thrown back, the chin uplifted, the large sweet human mouth, parted, showed small even teeth. The eyebrows were heavy, the nose straight and tilted, the complexion ivory-white, luminous, and sufficiently coloured.

As she saw Hastings, she rose at once and motioned her group aside.

"Whatever made you so late?" she exclaimed. "And this is Mr. Thorpe? I am so relieved that you have not been garotted, or blown into the bay. Captain Hastings is always the first to arrive and the last to leave — I was sure something had happened."

"You look remarkably worried," murmured Hastings.

"I cannot depress my other guests. They also have their rights." She gave Thorpe a gracious smile. "I have saved the fifth dance from this for you, and you are also to take me in to supper. Now I must go. *Hasta luego!* Captain Hastings, as it 's all your fault, I shall not give you a dance till after supper."

She spun down the room in the clasp of an army officer little taller than herself. Thorpe's eyes followed the fluent pair darting through the mob of dancers with the skill and energy of that time. Miss Randolph's eyes glittered, her little feet twinkled. She looked the integer of happy youth; and Thorpe turned away with a sigh, feeling old for the moment under the pressure of his large experience of the great world beyond California. He became aware that Hastings was introducing him to several men, and a moment later was guided to the library to have a drink. When he returned, it was time to claim Miss Randolph.

"Do you care to dance?" he asked as he plied her fan awkwardly. "I am rather rusty. To tell the truth, it 's eight years since I last danced, and I never was very keen on it. I should say that I 've been travelling a lot, and when I 'm home I go in for sport rather more than for the social taxes."

"What a relief to find a man who does n't dance! Let us go into the conservatory. Have you been much in America? How is it that you and Captain Hastings are such great friends?"

"He came over when a lad to visit some English relatives whose place adjoins ours, and we hit it off. Since then I have visited him in Louisiana, and we have travelled in Europe together."

"I suppose he amuses you — you are certainly unlike enough."

"Not in the least — he 's the prince of good fellows. What a jolly place!"

They had passed through the library and entered the conservatory: a small forest of palms, great ferns, and young orange-trees; brought, Miss Randolph explained, from Southern California. Chinese lanterns swung overhead. Rustic chairs and sofas, covered with the skins of panthers, wild cats, and coyotes, were grouped with much discretion.

Miss Randolph threw herself into a chair and let her head drop against the yellow skin on the back. Thorpe drew his chair close in front of her. In a moment he discovered that her lids were inclined to droop, and that there were lines about her mouth.

"You are tired," he said abruptly. "Shall I fetch you a glass of champagne?"

"Oh, no; it would n't do me a bit of good. Hot rooms and dancing always tire me. I 'm glad when the season is over. In another month or so we shall be going to Redwoods, our country home — about thirty miles south of San Francisco. You must come down with us; we have good shooting, — deer and quail in the mountains, and snipe and duck in the marshes."

"You are very kind," he said, and his reply was as mechanical as her invitation. He knew that all but the edge of her mind was turned from him, and was sufficiently interested to wish to get down into her thought. He went on gropingly: "I will confide to you that army life bores me a good deal, and as I intend to spend six months in California, I shall travel about somewhat." Then he added abruptly: "You are utterly unlike an English girl."

"I am a Californian. Blood does not go for much in this climate. You'll understand why, if you stay here long enough."

"In what way is it so unlike other places? I feel the difference, but cannot define it."

"It's the wickedest place on earth! I suppose there are wicked people everywhere, but California is a sort of headquarters. It seems to be a magnet for that element in human nature. I wish I had been born and brought up in England."

"Why?" he asked, smiling but puzzled, and recalling Hastings' imaginings. "I never saw any one look less wicked than yourself. Are you wicked?" he added, audaciously.

She flirted her fan at him, and her eyes danced so coquettishly that he no longer saw the drooping lids. "*Our* wickedness takes the form of flirtation,—heartless and unprincipled. Ask Captain Hastings. We are all refusing him in turn. Talk to me about England, while I study you and determine which line to take. I have n't typed you yet—I never make the fatal mistake of generalising."

As he answered the questions she put to him in rapid succession, his own impressions changed several times. He was charmed by her intelligence, occasionally by a flash of something deeper. Again, he saw only the thrilling beauty of her figure, and once something vibrated across his brain so fleeting that he barely realised it was an echo of the repulsion her mother had inspired.

"Well? What are your conclusions?" she demanded suddenly.

"I — what?"

"You have been sizing me up. I want to know the result."

"You shall not," he said stubbornly. "I — I beg pardon; I have lost the knack of polite fencing."

"I had read that Englishmen were blunt and truthful beings — either through conscious superiority or lack of complexity, I forget which. My father and the few others out here are almost denationalised."

"Well, I did beg pardon. And when a man is talking and receiving impressions at the same time, the impressions are not very well defined."

"But you think quickly and jump at conclusions. And minds of that sort sometimes make mistakes."

"I frequently make mistakes. Among the few things I have learned is not to judge people at sight — nor in a lifetime, for that matter. I certainly don't pretend to size up women, particularly women like yourself."

"That was very neat. Why myself? I am a very transparent young person." She flirted her lashes at him, but he fancied he saw a gleam of defiance shoot between them.

"You are not transparent. If you are kind enough to let me see a good deal of you, I fancy I shall know something of twenty Miss Randolphs by the time I leave California."

"Some you will like, and some you will not," she replied, with calm disregard of her previous assertion. "Well, I shall know what you think of me before long — don't make any mistake about that. Shall we flirt, by the way, or shall we merely be friends?"

"The last condition would give greater range to your inherent wickedness."

She laughed, apparently with much amusement. "I have a good many friends, nevertheless,—real friends. I have made it my particular art, and have rules and regulations. When they transgress, I fine them."

"Suppose we begin that way. I 'd like to know the rules."

"N-o, I don't think I want to. You see, the rule I most strictly enforce is that when the party of the other part transgresses, I never sit with him in a conservatory again."

"Let us cut the rules by all means. I feel a poor helpless male, quite at your mercy: I have n't been in a conservatory for years. Although I 've made a point of seeing something of the society of every capital I 've visited, I 've forgotten the very formula of flirtation. I might take a few lessons of Hastings —"

"Oh, don't! What a combination that would be! I will teach you all that it is necessary for you to know."

"Heaven help me. I shall be wise and sad when I leave California. However, I face my fate like a man; whatever happens, I shall not run. Just now it is my duty to wait on you. Shall I bring your supper here?"

"Yes — do. You will find a table behind that palm. Draw it up. There. Now bring what you like for yourself, but only a few oysters for me."

He returned in a few moments followed by a man, who spread the table with delicate fare.

Miss Randolph nibbled her oysters prettily. Thorpe was about to fill her glass with champagne, when she shook her head.

"I cannot," she said. "It goes to my head — one drop."

"Then don't, by all means. I hope you like it, and are resisting a temptation."

"I detest it, as it happens. If you want to see me in the high heroic rôle, which I infer you admire, you must devise a temptation of another sort."

"I think your dear little sex should be protected from all temptation. I rather like the Oriental way of doing things."

"Don't you flatter yourself that a wall fifteen feet high, and covered with broken glass, would protect a woman from temptations, if she wanted them. A man, to keep a woman inside that wall, must embody all the temptations himself."

Thorpe looked at her, and drew his brows together.

"That was a curious remark for a girl to make," he said, coldly.

"You mean it would be if I were English. But I am not only American, but Californian, born and brought up in a city where they are trying to be civilised and succeeding indifferently well. Do you suppose I can help seeing what life is? I should be next door to an idiot if I could."

"I hardly know whether you would be more interesting if you had been brought up in England. No," he added, reflectively, after a moment, "I don't think you would be."

"What you really think is, that I should not be half so interesting, but much more ideal."

"If I thought anything of the sort, it was by a purely mechanical process," he said, reddening. "I have lived out of England too much to be insular in all my notions."

"I don't believe an Englishman ever changes on certain points, of which woman is one; heredity is too strong. If you sat down and thought it all over, you'd find that although you could generalise on a more liberal scale than some of your countrymen, your own personal ideals were much the same as theirs."

"Possibly, but as I don't intend to marry till I'm forty, — when I intend to stand for Parliament, — I'm not bothering about ideals at present."

"That was a more insular remark than you evidently imagine. However — speaking of ideals, I should say that California generated them more liberally than any other country — through sheer force of contrast. I have grown rather morbid on the subject of good people, myself. I grow more exacting every month of my life; and the first thing I look for in a new man's face is to see, first, whether he has a mind, and then, whether it controls all the rest of him. I've seen too much of practical life to have indulged much in dreams and heroes; but I've let my imagination go somewhat, and I picture a man with all the virtues that you don't see in combination out here, and living with him in some old European city where there are narrow crooked streets, and beautiful architecture, and the most exquisite music in the cathedrals."

Her voice had rattled on lightly, and she smiled more than once during her long speech. But her eyes did not smile; they had a curious, almost hard, intentness which forced Thorpe to believe that her brain was casting up something more than the froth of a passing mood.

"I am afraid you won't meet your hero of all the virtues," he said, "even in a picturesque old continental town. But I think I understand your feeling. It is the principle of good in you demanding its proper companionship and setting."

"Yes, that is it," she said, softly. "That is it. I am no worse than other girls; but I flirt and waste my time abominably. It would be all right if I did no more thinking than they do; but I do so much that, if I were inclined to be religious, I believe I 'd run, one of these days, into a convent. However, I can always look forward to the old European town."

"Alone?"

"I suppose when your left eyebrow goes up like that you 're trying to flirt. I don't know that I 'd mind being alone, particularly.

It would be several thousand times better than the society of some of the people I 've been forced to associate with. I love art, — particularly architecture and music, — and I 'm sure I could weave a romance round myself. Yes, I 'm sure I should love it as much as I hate this country," she added with such vehemence that Thorpe set down his fork abruptly.

"You are very pale," he said; "I think you had better take a little champagne. Indeed, you must be utterly worn out. I can imagine what a lot you have had to do and think of to-day."

He filled her glass, and she drank the champagne quickly.

"I have a shocking head," she said; "but I *need* this. I have been out eight nights in succession, and have been on the go all day besides. Mother never attends to anything; and father, of course, is too busy to bother with parties. Cochrane and I have to do everything."

"Tell me some more of your ideals," said Thorpe. He was not sure that he liked her, but she piqued his curiosity.

"Ideals? Who ever had an ideal after a glass of champagne — except to be in the wildest spirits for the rest of one's life? There will be no champagne in Bruges — that's the city I've settled on; but I can't even think of Bruges. Champagne suggests Paris, and they tell me Paris is even more wicked than San Francisco. Is it?"

Her eyes were sparkling with merriment; but although she refilled her glass, there was no suggestion as yet of the bacchante about her. The colour had come back to her face, and she looked very charming. Nevertheless Thorpe frowned and shook his head.

"I should prefer to talk about Bruges," he said. "I've been there, and can tell you all you'd like to know. When I go back, I'll send you some photographs."

"Thanks — but I have a whole portfolio full. I want to hear about Paris. I'm afraid you're a bit of a prig."

"No man could be less of a prig. I hope you are above the silly idea that, because we English have a slightly higher standard than other nations, it follows that we are prigs. You were entirely delightful a few moments ago; but I don't like to see a woman drink when it affects her as it does you."

The colour flew from her cheeks to her hair, and her eyes flashed angrily. "You *are* a prig, and you are extremely impertinent," she said.

Thorpe sprang to his feet, plunging his hands into his pockets.

"Oh — don't — don't — " he exclaimed. "I'm afraid I was rude. I assure you, I did not intend to criticise you. Please say you forgive me."

She smiled and shrugged her shoulders. "You look so really penitent," she said gaily. "Sit down and fill my glass, and drink to our — friendship."

He was about to remonstrate; but reflecting that it would be a bore to apologise twice in succession, and also that what she did was none of his affair, he filled her glass. She touched it to his, and threw herself back against the skins, sipping the wine slowly and chattering nonsense. He refilled her glass absently the fourth time; but when she pushed it across the table again, he said, with some decision;

"Be careful. This champagne is very heady. I feel it myself."

She drained the glass. For a moment they stared hard at each other in silence, Thorpe wondering at the sudden maturity in the face before him. All the triumphant young womanhood had gone out of it; the diabolical spirit of some ancestor entombed in the depths of her brain might have possessed her for the moment, smothering her own groping soul. The distant music filled the conservatory with a low humming sound, such as one hears in a tropical forest at noon. Suddenly Thorpe realised that the evil which is in all human souls was having its moment of absolute liberty, and that the two dissevered particles, his and hers, recognised each other. He had knocked his senseless many times in his life, but he felt no inclination to do so to-night; for so much more than what little was evil in this girl attracted and magnetised him. His brain was not clear, and it was reckless with its abrupt possession by the idea that this woman was his mate, and that, for good or for evil, there was no escaping her. He sprang to his feet, pushed the table violently aside, took her in his arms and kissed her. For a moment she was quiescent; then she slipped from his embrace and ran down the conservatory, thrusting the ferns aside. One fell, its jar crashing on the stone floor. He saw no more of her that night.

II

Two days later Thorpe was strolling up and down the beach before the Presidio. The plaza was deserted; here and there, on the verandahs of the low adobe houses surrounding it, officers lay at full length in hammocks, smoking or reading, occasionally flirting with some one in white.

Every trace of the storm had fled. The warmth and fragrance and restlessness of spring were in the air. The bay, as calm as a mountain lake, reflected a deep blue sky with no wandering white to give it motion. Outside the Golden Gate, the spray leaped high, and the ocean gave forth its patient roar. The white sails on the bay hung limply. Opposite was a line of steep cliffs, bare and green; beyond was a stupendous peak, dense and dark with redwoods. Farther down, facing the young city, hills jutted, romantic with sweeping willows. Between was the solitary rock, Alcatraz, with its ugly fort of many eyes. Far to the east was a line of pink mountains dabbled with blue, tiny villages clinging to their knees.

Thorpe's keen eye took in every detail. It pleased him more than anything he had seen for some time. After a long rainy day in quarters, trying to talk nonsense to the Presidio women in their cramped parlours, and giving his opinion of California some thirty times, he felt that he could hail the prospect of a week of fresh air and solitude with the enthusiasm of a schoolboy. He kept the tail of his eye on the square, ready to hasten his steps and disappear round the sand dunes, did any one threaten to intrude upon his musings.

He saw a man ride into the plaza, dismount at the barracks, and a moment later head for the beach. Thorpe's first impulse was to flee. But he stopped short; he had recognised Mr. Randolph's butler.

The man touched his hat as he approached. "A note from Miss Randolph, sir."

Thorpe opened the note. It read:

MY DEAR MR. THORPE, — I should like to see you this afternoon, if you are disengaged. If not, at your earliest convenience. I hope you will understand that this is not an idle request, but that I particularly wish to see you.

Sincerely,

NINA RANDOLPH.

"Tell Miss Randolph that I will call at three," said Thorpe, promptly.

He had no wish to avoid the interview; he was quite willing that she should turn the scorpions of her wrath upon him. He deserved it. He did not pretend to understand Nina Randolph, deeply as he had puzzled over her since their memorable interview; but that he had helped her to violate her own self-respect, there could be little doubt, and he longed to give her what satisfaction he could. He had lived his inner life very fully, and knew all that the sacrifice of an ideal meant to the higher parts of the mind. Whether Miss Randolph had ever kissed a man before or not, he would not pretend to guess; but he would have been willing to swear that she had never kissed another in the same circumstances; and he burned to think that he had been the man to cast her at the foot of her girlish pedestal. Whatever possibilities for evil there might be in her, instinct prompted him to believe that they were undeveloped. Her strong sudden magnetism for him had passed with her presence, and, looking back, he attributed it entirely to the momentary passion of which he was ashamed; but he felt something of the curious tie which binds thinking people who have helped each other a step down the moral ladder.

After luncheon, he informed Hastings that he was going to the city, and asked for a horse.

"I'll go with you —"

"I don't want you," said Thorpe, bluntly. "I have a particular reason for wishing to go alone."

"Oh, very well," said Hastings, amiably. "The savage loves his solitude, I know."

The road between the army posts and

San Francisco was well beaten. Thorpe could not have lost his way, even if the horse had not known every inch of it.

He reached the city within an hour. It was less picturesque by day than by night. The board sidewalks were broken and uneven, the streets muddy. The tall frame buildings of the business section looked as if they had been pieced together in intervals between gambling and lynching. Dwelling-houses with gardens about them were scattered on the heights.

Two miles south of the swarming, hurrying, swearing brain of the city was the aristocratic quarter,—South Park and Rincon Hill. The square wooden houses, painted a dark brown, had a solid and substantial air, and looked as if they might endure through several generations.

The man, Cochrane, admitted Thorpe, and conducted him to the library. The room was unoccupied, and, as the door closed behind the butler, Thorpe for the first time experienced a flutter. He was about to have a serious interview with a girl of whose type he knew nothing. Would she expect him to apologise?

He had always held that the man who kissed and apologised was an ass. But he had done Miss Randolph something more than a minor wrong.

He shrugged his shoulders and took his stand before the fireplace. She had sent for him; let her take the initiative. He knew woman well enough to follow her cues, be the type new or old. Then he looked about him with approval. One would know it was an Englishman's library, he thought. Book-shelves, closely furnished, lined two sides of the large and lofty room. One end opened into the conservatory — where palms did shelter and the lights were dim. The rugs and curtains were red, the furniture very comfortable. On a long table were the periodicals of the world.

Miss Randolph kept him waiting but a few moments. She opened the door abruptly and entered. Her face was pale, and her eyes were shadowed; but she held her head very high. Her carriage and her long dark gown made her appear almost tall. As she advanced down the room, she looked at Thorpe steadily, without access of colour, her lips pressed together. He met her half way. His first impression was that her figure was the most beautiful he had ever seen, his next the keenest impulse of pity he had felt for any woman.

She extended her hand mechanically, and he took it and held it.

"Is it true that I kissed you the other night?" she asked, peremptorily.

"Yes," he said, ungracefully.

"And I had drunk too much champagne?"

"It was my fault," he said, eagerly. "You told me that you had a bad head. I had no business to press it on you."

"You must think I am a poor weak creature indeed, if my friends are obliged to take care of me," she said drily. "I was a fool to touch it—that is the long and the short of it. I have given you a charming impression of the girls of San Francisco—sit down: we look idiotic standing in the middle of the room holding each other's hand—I can assure you that there was not another girl in the house who would have done what I did, or whom you would have dared to kiss. In a new country, you know, the social lines are drawn very tight, and the best people are particular to prudery. It is necessary: there are so many dreadful women out here. I am positive that in the set to which Captain Hastings has introduced you, you will meet a larger number of well-conducted people than you have ever met in any one place before."

"It is very good of you to put on armour for your city," he said, smiling. "I shall always think of it as your city, by the way. But I thought you did not like California."

"It is my country. I feel great pride in it. You will find that it is a country with a peculiar influence. Some few natures it leaves untouched—but they are precious few. In the others, it quickens all the good and evil they were born with."

Thorpe looked at her with a profound interest. He was eager to hear all that she had to say.

"I have never before had occasion to speak like this to any man," she went on. "If I had had, I should not have done so. I should have carried it off with a high hand, ignored it, assumed that I was above criticism.

I only speak to you so frankly because you are an Englishman. People of the same blood are clannish when away from their own land. I say this without coquetry: I care more for your good opinion than for that of any of the others — I am so tired of them!"

"Thank you — even if you did rather spoil it. You have it, if it really matters to you. Surely, you don't think I misunderstand. I insist upon assuming all the blame — and — upon apologising."

"Well, I am glad you apologised. Although you were not the most to blame, just for the moment it made me feel that you were. I have already forgiven you." She dropped her eyes for a moment, then looked at him again with her square, almost defiant regard. "There is something I have been trying to lead up to. It is this — it is not very easy to say — I want you to make a promise. There is a skeleton in this house. Some people know. I don't want you to ask them about it. My father will ask you here constantly. I shall want you to come, too. I ask you to promise to keep your eyes shut. Will you?"

"I shall see nothing. Thanks, thanks." He got up and moved nervously about. "We will be friends, the best of friends, promise me that. No flirtation. No nonsense. There may be something I can do to help you while I am here. I hope there will be."

"There will not, but I like you better for saying that — I know you are not demonstrative." She threw herself back in her chair and smiled charmingly. "As to the other part — yes, we shall be the best of friends. It was hard to speak, but I am glad that I did. I knew it was either that or a nodding acquaintance, and I had made up my mind that it should be something quite different. When we are alone and serious, we will not flirt; but I have moods, irrepressible ones. If, when we meet in society, I happen to be in a highly flirtatious humour, you are to flirt with me. Do you understand?"

"Certainly, certainly, I agree — to keep you from flirting with other men."

"Now fetch that portfolio over there, — it has Bruges in it, — and tell me something about every stone."

They talked for two hours, and of much beside Bruges. Haphazardly as she had been educated in this new land, her natural intelligence had found nutrition in her father's mind and library. Thorpe noted that when talking on subjects which appealed to the intellect alone, her face changed strikingly: the heavy lids lifted, the eyes sparkled coldly, the mouth lost its full curves. Even her voice, so warm and soft, became, more than once, harsh and sharp.

"There are several women in her," he thought. "She certainly is very interesting. I should like to meet her again ten years hence."

He did.

"Why don't you travel?" he asked. "It would mean so much more to you than to most women. Even if Mr. Randolph cannot leave this fair young city he is building up, and your mother won't leave him, you could go with some one else —"

"I never expect to leave California," she said shortly. Then, as she met his look of surprise, she added: "I told you a fib when I said that I did not dream, or only a little.

I get out of my own life for hours at a time by imagining myself in Europe, cultivating my mind, my taste for art, to their utmost limit, living a sort of impersonal life — Of course there are times when I imagine myself with some one who would care for it all as much as I, and know more — and all that. But I try to keep to the other. I have suffered enough to know that in the impersonal life is the surest content. And as for the other — it could not be, even if I ever met such a man. But dreams help one enormously, and I am the richer for all I have indulged in."

Thorpe stood up again. Under a rather impassive exterior, he was a restless man, and his acquaintance with Nina Randolph had tried his nerves.

"I wish you had not given me half confidences, or that you would refrain from rousing my curiosity — my interest, as you do. It is hardly fair. I don't wish to know what the family skeleton is, but I do want to know *you* better. If you want the truth, I have never been so *intrigué* by a woman in my life. And I have never so wanted to help one. I have been so drawn to you that I have had a sense of having done you a personal wrong ever since the other night. A man does not usually feel that way when he kisses a girl. I see it is no use to ask your confidence now; but, mind, I don't say I sha'n't demand it later on."

At this moment the butler entered with the lamps. He was followed immediately by Mr. Randolph, who exclaimed delightedly:

"Is it really you, Mr. Thorpe? I have just sent you a note asking you to dine with us on Sunday. And you'll stay to dinner to-night — no, I won't listen to any excuses. If you knew what a pleasure it is to meet an Englishman once more!"

"Hastings will think I am lost —"

"I'll send him a note, and ask him to come in for the evening, and I'll get in a dozen of our neighbours. We'll have some music and fun."

"Very well — I am rather keen on staying, to tell you the truth. Many thanks."

"Sit down. You must see something of sport here. It is very interesting in this wild country."

"I should like it above all things." Thorpe sat forward eagerly, forgetting Miss Randolph.

"What have you that's new? I've killed pretty nearly everything."

"We will have an elk hunt."

"I want to go, too," said Nina, authoritatively.

Thorpe turned, and smiled, as he saw the hasty retreat of an angry sparkle.

"I am afraid you would be a disturbing influence," he said gallantly.

"I should n't disturb you," she said, with the pertness of a spoilt child. "I am a good shot myself. I can go — can't I, papa?"

Mr. Randolph smiled indulgently. "You can do anything you like, my darling," he said. "I wonder you condescend to ask."

Nina ran over and kissed him, then propped her chin on top of his head and looked defiantly at Thorpe.

"If you don't take me," she remarked, drily, "there will be no hunt."

"On the whole, I think my mind would concentrate better if you were not absent," he said.

She blew him a kiss. "You *are* improving. *Hastu luego!* I must go and smooth my feathers." And she ran out of the room.

The two men talked of the threatened civil upheaval in the United States until dinner was announced, a half hour later.

Mrs. Randolph did not appear until the soup had been removed. She entered the dining-room hurriedly, muttering an apology. Her toilette had evidently been made in haste: her brooch was awry; and her hair, banded down the face after the fashion of the time, hung an inch below one ear and exposed the lobe of the other, dealing detrimentally with her dignity, despite her fine physique.

She took no part in the conversation for some time. It was very lively. Mr. Randolph was full of anecdote and information, and enjoyed scintillating. He frequently referred to Nina, as if proud of her cleverness and anxious to exhibit it; but the guest noticed that he never addressed a word—nor a glance—to his wife.

Suddenly Thorpe's eyes rested on a small dark painting in oils, the head of an old man.

"That is rather good," he said, "and a very interesting face."

"You have probably never heard of the artist, unless you have read the life of his sister. I was so fond of the man that I resent his rescue from oblivion by the fame of a woman. His name was Branwell Brontë, and that is a portrait of my grandfather."

"If Branwell 'ad a-conducted hisself," said a heavy voice opposite, "'ee 'd a-been the wonder of the family. Mony a time a 've seen 'im coom into tha Lord Rodney Inn, 'is sharp little face as red as tha scoollery maid's 'ands, and rockin' from one side of tha 'all to tha hother, and sit doon at tha table, and make a carica*chure* of ivvery mon thot coom in. And once when 'ee was station-master at Luddondon Foote a 've 'eard as 'ow a mon coom runnin' oop just as tha train went oot, and said as 'ow 'ee was horful anxious to know if a certain mon went hoff. 'Ee tried describin' 'im, and could n't, so Branwell drew pictures of all the persons as 'ad left, and 'ee recog*nised* the one as 'ee wanted."

There was a moment's silence, so painful that Thorpe felt his nerves jumping and the colour rising to his face. He recalled his promise, and looked meditatively at the strange concoction which had been placed before him as Mrs. Randolph finished. But his thought was arbitrary. An ignorant woman of the people, possibly an ex-servant, who could only play the gentlewoman through a half-dozen rehearsed sentences, and forget the rôle completely at times! He had not expected to find the skeleton so soon.

"That is *carne con agi*, a Chile dish," said Mr. Randolph, suavely. "I 'm very fond of Spanish cooking, myself, and you had better begin your education in it at once: you will get a good deal out here."

"I am jolly glad to hear it. I 'm rather keen on new dishes." He glanced up. Mr. Randolph was yellow. The lines in his face had deepened. Thorpe dared not look at Nina.

III

Some eight or ten people, including Hastings, came in after dinner. Mrs. Randolph had gone upstairs from the dining-room, and did not appear again. Her dampening influence removed, Mr. Randolph and Nina recovered their high light spirits; and there was much music and more conversation. Miss Randolph had a soprano voice of piercing sweetness, which flirted effectively with Captain Hastings' tenor. Thorpe thought Hastings an ass for rolling his eyes out of his head, and finally turned his back on the piano to meet the large amused glance of Miss Hathaway. He sat down beside her, and, being undisturbed for ten minutes, found her willing to converse, or rather to express a number of decided opinions. She told him whom he was to know, what parts of California he was to visit, how long he was to stay, and after what interval he was to return. Thorpe listened with much entertainment, for her voice was not tuned to friendly advice, but to command. Her great eyes were as cold as icicles under a blue light; but there was a certain cordiality in their invitation to flirt. Thorpe did not respond. If he had known her first, he reflected, he should doubtless have made an attempt to dispossess her court; but the warm magnetic influence of Nina Randolph held him, strengthened by her demand upon his sympathy. Still he felt that Miss Hathaway was a person to like, and remained at her side until he was dismissed in favour of Hastings; when he talked for a time to the intellectual Miss McDermott, the sweet and slangy Miss McAllister, who looked like an angel and talked like a gamin, to Don Roberto Yorba, a handsome and exquisitely attired little grandee who was trying to look as much like an American as his friend Hiram Polk, with his lantern jaws and angular figure. It was the first city Thorpe had visited where there was no type: everybody suggested being the father or mother of one, and was of an individuality so pronounced that the stranger marvelled they were not all at one another's throats. But he had never seen people more amiable and fraternal.

He did not see Nina alone again until a few moments before he left. He drew her out into the hall while Hastings was saying good-night to Mr. Randolph.

"May I come often?" he asked.

"*Will* you?"

"I certainly shall."

"Will you talk to me about things that men scarcely ever talk to girls about,— books and art — and — what one thinks about more than what one does."

"I 'll talk about anything under heaven that

you want to talk about — particularly yourself."

"I don't want to talk about myself."

Her face was sparkling with coquetry, but it flushed under the intensity of his gaze. His brown skin was paler than when he had entered the house, his hard features were softened by the shaded lamp of the hall, and his grey eyes had kindled as he took her hand. She looked very lovely in a white gown touched up with red velvet bows.

"I believe you'll be a tremendous flirt by the time you leave here," she said, trying to draw her hand away. "And don't tell me this is your first experience in eight years."

"I've known a good many women," he said, bluntly. "At present I am only following your cues — and there are a bewildering lot of them. When you are serious, I shall be serious. When you are not — I shall endeavour to be frivolous. To be honest, however, I have no intention of flirting with you, fascinating and provocative as you are. I'd like awfully to be your intimate friend, but nothing more. Good-night."

IV

South Park in the Fifties and Sixties was the gayest quarter of respectable San Francisco, with not a hint of the gloom which now presses about it like a pall. The two concave rows of houses were the proudest achievements of Western masonry, and had a somewhat haughty air, as if conscious of the importance they sheltered. The inner park was green and flowered; the flag of the United States floated proudly above. The whole precinct had that atmosphere of happy informality peculiar to the brief honeymoon of a great city. People ran, hatless, in and out of each other's houses, and sat on the doorsteps when the weather was fine. The present aristocracy of San Francisco, the landed gentry of California whose coat-of-arms should be a cocktail, a side of mutton, or a dishonest contract, would give not a few of their dollars for personal memories of that crumbling enclosure at the foot of the hill: memories that would be welcome even with the skeleton which, rambling through these defaced abandoned houses, they might expect to see grinning in dark spidery corners or in rat-claimed cupboards. Poor old houses! They have kept silent and faithful guard over the dark tales and tragic secrets of their youth; curiosity has been forced to satisfy itself with little more than vague and ugly rumour. The memories that throng them tell little to any but the dead.

There lived, in those days, the Randolphs, the Hathaways, the Dom Pedro Earles, the Hunt McLanes, the three families to which the famous "Macs" belonged, and others that have no place in this story. Before his second week in California was finished, Thorpe knew them all, and was petted and made much of; for San Francisco, then as now, dearly loved the aristocratic stranger. He rode into the city every day, either alone or with Hastings, and rarely returned without spending several moments or hours with Nina Randolph. Sometimes she was alone, sometimes companioned by her intimate friend, Molly Shropshire, — a large masculine girl of combative temper and imbued with disapproval of man. She made no exception in favour of Thorpe, and when he did not find her in the way, he rather enjoyed quarrelling with her. Mrs. Randolph made no more abrupt incursions into the table talk and spent most of her time in her room. Occasionally Thorpe met in the hall a coarse-looking woman whom he knew to be a Mrs. Reinhardt and the favoured friend of Mrs. Randolph. Mr. Randolph was often in brilliant spirits; at other times he looked harassed and sad; but he always made Thorpe feel the welcome guest.

Thorpe, during the first fortnight of their acquaintance, snubbed his maiden attempt to understand Nina Randolph; it was so evident that she did not wish to be understood that he could but respect her reserve. Besides, she was the most charming woman in the place, and that was enough to satisfy any visitor. Just after that he began to see her alone every day; Miss Shropshire had retired to the obscuriry of her chamber with a cold, and socialities rarely began before night. They took long walks together in the wild environs of the city, once or twice as far as the sea. Both had a high fine taste in literature, and she was eager for the books of travel he had lived. He sounded her, to discover if she had ambition, for she was an imperious little queen in society; but she convinced him that, when alone or with him, she rose high above the petty strata of life. With a talent, she could have been one of the most rapt and impersonal slaves of Art the world had ever known; and, as it was, her perception for beauty was extraordinary. Thorpe wished that she could carry out her imaginings and live a life of study in Europe; it seemed a great pity that she should marry and settle down into a mere leader of society.

Toward the end of the second fortnight, he began to wonder whether he should care to marry her, were he ready for domesticity, and were there no disquieting mystery about her. He concluded that he should not, as he should doubtless be insanely in love with her if he loved her at all, and she was too various of mood for a man's peace of mind. But in the wake of these reflections came the impulse to analyse her, and he made no further attempt to snub it.

He went one evening to the house of Mrs. Hunt McLane, a beautiful young Creole who held the reins of the infant city's society in her small determined hands. Born into the aristocracy of Louisiana, she had grown up in the salon. Her husband had arrived in San Francisco at the period when a class of rowdies known as "The Hounds" were terrorising the city, and, when they were finally arrested and brought to trial, conducted the prosecution. The brilliant legal talent he displayed, the tremendous personal force which carried every jury he addressed, established his position at the head of the bar at once. His wife, with her wide knowledge of the world, her tact, magnetism, and ambition, found no one to dispute her social leadership.

As Thorpe entered, she was standing at the head of the long parlour; and with her high-piled hair, *poudré*, her gown of dark-red velvet, and her haughty carriage, she looked as if she had just stepped from an old French canvas.

She smiled brilliantly as Thorpe approached her, and he was made to feel himself the guest of the evening,—a sensation he shared with every one in the room.

"I have not seen you for three days and

seven hours," she said. "How are all your flirtations getting on?"

"All my what?"

"Dominga Earle is making frantic eyes at you," indicating, with a rapid motion of her pupils, a tall slender Mexican who undulated like a snake and whose large black fan and eyes were never idle. "'Lupie Hathaway is looking coldly expectant; and Nina Randolph, who was wholly animated a moment ago, is now quite listless. Not that you are to feel particularly flattered; you are merely something new. Turn over the pages,—Dominga is going to sing,—and I am convinced that she will surpass herself."

Mrs. Earle was swaying on the piano stool. Her black eyes flashed a welcome to Thorpe, as he moved obediently to her side. Then she threw back her head, raised her eyebrows, dilated her nostrils, and in a ringing contralto sang a Spanish love-song. Thorpe could not understand a word of it, but inferred that it was passionate from the accompaniment of glance which played between himself and a tall blonde man leaning over the piano.

When the song and its encore finished, she

was immediately surrounded, and Thorpe slipped away. Miss Randolph was barricaded. He went over to Miss Hathaway, who sat between Hastings and another officer, *looking* impartially at each. They were dismissed in a manner which made them feel the honour of her caprice.

"That was good of you," said Thorpe, sinking into a chair opposite her. "It is rarely that one can get a word with you, merely a glance over three feet of shoulder."

Miss Hathaway made no reply. It was one of her idiosyncrasies never to take the slightest notice of a compliment. She was looking very handsome, although her attire, as ever, suggested a cold disregard of the looking-glass. Thorpe, who was beginning to understand her, did not feel snubbed, but fell to wondering what sort of a time Hastings would have of it when he proposed.

She regarded him meditatively for a moment, then remarked: "You are absent-minded to-night, and that makes you look rather stupid."

Again Thorpe was not disconcerted. Speeches of this sort from Miss Hathaway were to be hailed as signs of favour. If she did not like a man, she did not talk to him at all. He might sit opposite her throughout the night, and she would not part her lips.

"I am stupid," he replied. "I have been all day."

"What is the matter?" Her voice did not soften as another woman's might have done, but it betrayed interest. "Are you puzzling?"

He coloured, nettled at her insight; but he answered, coldly: —

"Yes; I am puzzling."

"Do not," said Miss Hathaway, significantly. "Puzzle about any one else in California, but not about Nina Randolph."

"What is this mystery?" he exclaimed impatiently, then added hastily, "oh, bother! I am too much of a wanderer to puzzle over any one."

Miss Hathaway fixed her large cold blue regard upon him. "Do you love Nina Randolph?" she asked.

"I am afraid I love all women too much to trust to my own selection of one."

"Now you are stupid. Go and talk to Nina." She turned her back upon him, and smiled indulgently to a new-comer.

He crossed the room; a group of men parted with indifferent grace, and he leaned over Nina's chair.

She was looking gay and free of care, and her eyes flashed a frank welcome to Thorpe. "I thought you were not coming to talk to me," she said, with a little pout.

"Duty first," he murmured. "Come over into the little reception-room and talk to me."

"What am I to do with all these men?"

"Nothing."

"You are very exacting — for a friend."

"If you are a good friend, you will come. I am tired and bored."

She rose, shook out her pretty pink skirts, nodded to her admirers, and walked off with Thorpe.

He laughed. "Perhaps they will console themselves with the reflection that as they have spoiled you, they should stand the consequences."

They took possession of a little sofa in the

reception-room. Another couple was in the window curve, and yet another opposite.

"We have not had our hunt," said Nina; "the country has been a mud-hole. But we are to have it on Monday, if all goes well."

"Who else is to be of the party?"

"Molly, Guadalupe, and Captain Hastings. Don't speak of it to any one else. I don't want a crowd."

She lay back, her skirts sweeping his feet. A pink ribbon was twisted in her hair. The colour in her cheeks was pink. The pose of her head, as she absently regarded the stupid frescoes on the ceiling, strained her beautiful throat, making it look as hard as ivory, accentuating the softer loveliness of the neck. Thorpe looked at her steadily. He rarely touched her hand.

"I have something else in store for you," she said, after a moment. "Just beyond the army posts are great beds of wild strawberries. It was a custom in the Spanish days to get up large parties every spring and camp there, gather strawberries, wander on the beach and over the hills, and picnic generally. We have kept it up; and if this weather lasts, if spring is really here, a crowd of us are going in a couple of weeks — you included. You have no idea what fun it is!"

"I shall not try to imagine it." He spoke absently. He was staring at a curling lock that had strayed over her temple. He wanted to blow it.

"I am tired," she said. "Talk to me. I have been gabbling for an hour."

"I 'm not in the mood for talking," he said, shortly. "But keep quiet, if you want to. I suppose we know each other well enough for that."

The other people left the room. Nina arranged herself more comfortably, and closed her eyes. Her mouth relaxed slightly, and Thorpe saw the lines about it. She looked older when the animation was out of her face, but none the less attractive. His eyes fell on her neck. He moved closer. She opened her eyes, and he raised his. The colour left her face, and she rose.

"Take me to papa," she said; "I am going home."

V

The party for the elk-hunt assembled at Mr. Randolph's door at four o'clock on Monday morning. Miss Hathaway's large Spanish eyes were heavy with the languor of her race. Miss Shropshire looked cross. Even the men were not wholly animate. Nina alone was as widely awake as the retreating stars. She rode ahead with Thorpe.

They made for the open country beyond the city. What is now a large and populous suburb, was then a succession of sand dunes, in whose valleys were thickets of scrub oak, chaparral, and willows. A large flat lying between Rincon Hill and Mission Bay was the favourite resort of elk, deer, antelope, and the less aristocratic coyote and wild cat. It was to this flat that Mr. Randolph's party took their way, accompanied by vaqueros leading horses upon which to bring back the spoils of the morning.

The hour was grey and cold. The landscape looked inexpressibly bleak. A blustering wind travelled between the sea and the bay. From the crests of the hills they had an occasional glimpse of water and of the delapidated Mission, solitary on its cheerless plain.. In the little valleys, the thickets were so dense they were obliged to bend their heads. The morning was intensely still, but for the soft pounding of the horses' hoofs on the yielding earth, the long despairing cry of the coyote, the sudden flight of a startled wild cat.

"We are all so modern, we seem out of place in this wilderness," said Thorpe. "I can hardly accept the prophecy of your father and other prominent men here, that San Francisco will one day be the great financial and commercial centre of Western America. It seems to me as hopeless as making cake out of bran."

"Just you wait," said Nina, tossing her head. "It will come in our time, in my father's time. You haven't got the feel of the place yet, haven't got it into your bones. And you don't know what we Californians can do, when we put our minds to it."

"I hope I shall see it," he replied, smiling; "I hope to see California at many stages of her growth. I am a nomad, you know, and I shall make it the objective point of my travels hereafter. The changes — I don't doubt if they come at all they will ride the lightning — will interest me deeply. May there be none in you," he added, gallantly. "I cannot imagine any."

Her eyes drooped, and her underlids pressed upward, — a repellant trick that had made Thorpe uncomfortable more than once. "That is where you will find the changes upon which the city will not pride itself," she said. "Fortunately, there won't be many of them."

"You are unfair," he said, angrily. "You told me to ask you no questions, and this is not the first time you have deliberately pricked my curiosity — that is not the word, either. The first night I dined at your house —" he stopped, biting his lip. He had said more than he intended.

"I know. You thought you had discovered the secret — I know exactly what you thought. But you have come to the conclusion since that there is more behind. Well, you are right."

"What is your secret? I have had opportunities to discover. I hope I need not tell you that I have shut my ears; but I wish you would tell me. I don't like mystery. It is sensational and old-fashioned. Between such friends as ourselves, it is entirely without excuse. It is more than possible that, girl-like, you have exaggerated its importance, and you are in danger of becoming morbid. But, whether it is real or imaginary, let me help you. Every woman needs a man's help, and you can have all of mine that you want. Only don't keep prodding my imagination, and telling me not to think. I am close upon thinking of nothing else."

"Well, just fancy that that is my way of making myself interesting; that I cannot help flirting a little, even with friends." She laughed lightly; but her face, which was not always under her control, had changed: it looked dull and heavy.

"That is pure nonsense," he said, shortly. "Do you suppose you make yourself more interesting by hinting that your city will one day be ashamed of you?"

"Ah, perhaps *that* was an exaggeration."

"I should hope so."

"I meant one's city need not know everything."

"You are unpleasantly perverse this morning. I choose to take what you said as an exaggeration; but there is something behind, and I feel strongly impelled to say that if you don't tell me I shall leave."

"If I did, you would take the next steamer."

"I am the one to decide that. At least give me the opportunity to reduce your mountain to a mole-hill."

"Even you could not. And look — I see no reason why friends should wish to get at one another's inner life. The companionship of friends is mental only. I have given you my mind freely. You have no right to ask for my soul. You are not my lover, and you don't wish to be, although I don't doubt that at times you imagine you do."

"I am free to confess that I have imagined it more than once. I will set the example by being perfectly frank with you. If I could understand you, if I were not tormented by all sorts of dreadful possibilities, I should have let myself go long before this. Does that sound cold-blooded? I can only say in explanation that I was born with a good deal of self-control, and that I have strengthened my will by exercise. It would be either one extreme or the other with me. At first I thought I should not want to marry you in any case. I am now sufficiently in love with you to long to be wholly so."

Nina stole a glance at him with a woman's uncontrollable curiosity, even in great moments. But he had turned his head from her, and was hitting savagely at his boot.

"I will be frank to this extent, by way of return: The barrier between us is insurmountable, and you would be the first to admit it. I will tell you the whole truth the day before you leave; that must content you. And, meanwhile, nip in the bud what is merely a compound of sympathy and passion. I know the influence I exert perfectly. I have seen more than one man go off his head. It humiliates me beyond expression."

"It need not—although it is extremely distasteful to me that you should have seen men go off their heads, as you express it,

But passion is the mightiest factor in love; there is no love without it, and it is bound to predominate until it is satisfied. Then the affections claim their part; and a dozen other factors, mental companionship for one, enter in. But, for Heaven's sake, don't add to your morbidity by despising yourself because you inspire passion in men. The women who do not are not worth considering."

"Is that true? Well, I am glad you have suggested another way of looking at it. I don't think I am morbid. At all events no one in this world ever made a harder fight not to be."

They were riding through a thicket, and he turned and brought his face so close to hers that she had only a flashing glimpse of its pallor and of the flame in his eyes.

"It is your constant fight that wrings my heart," he said. "Whatever it is against, I will make it with you, if you will let me. I am strong enough for both. And who am I that I should judge you? I have not lived the life of a saint. We all have our ideals. Mine has been never to give way except when I chose, never to let my senses control my mind for an instant. I believe, therefore, that I am strong enough to help and protect you against everything. And, whatever it is, you shall never be judged by me."

They left the thicket at the moment, and she pushed her horse aside, that she might no longer feel Thorpe's touch, his breath on her neck. "You are the most generous of men," she said; "and you can have the satisfaction of knowing that you have made me think better of myself and of human nature than I have ever thought before. But I cannot marry you. Not only is the barrier insurmountable, but I don't love you. Here we are."

VI

THORPE at this time spent few hours in his own company. There was abundant distraction: either a social entertainment every day or evening, or a lark in the city. The wild life about the plaza, the gambling houses, the saloons, the fatal encounters in the dark contiguous streets, the absolute recklessness of the men and women, interested him profoundly. As he spent money freely, and never passed a gaming table without tossing down a handful of coin as ardently as any adventurer, he was popular, and free to come and go as he liked.

The scene which he most frequented, which rose most vividly when he was living his later life in England, was El Dorado. It had three great windows on the plaza and six in its length, — something over a hundred and twenty feet. The brilliant and extraordinary scene within was visible to those who shunned it but stood with a fascinated stare; for its curtains were never drawn, its polished windows were close upon the sidewalk. On one side, down its entire length, was a bar set with expensive crystal, over which passed every variety of drink known to the appetite of man. Behind the bar were mirrors from floor to ceiling, reflecting the room, doubling the six crystal blazing chandeliers, the forty or fifty tables piled high with gold and silver, the hard intent faces of the gamblers, the dense throng that ever sauntered in the narrow aisles. At the lower end was a platform on which musicians played droning tunes on hurdy-gurdies, and Mexican girls, who looked like devils, danced. In the middle of the platform, awaiting the counters of the patrons of the bar, one woman sat always. She was French, and dark, and handsome, and weighed three hundred pounds. Dressing such a person was expensive in those days of incredible prices, and that room was very warm; she wore but a yard or two of silk somewhere about the belt.

Thorpe often sat and watched the faces of the gamblers: the larger number were gently born, and more than one told him that he had been a schoolmaster, a college professor, a clergyman, a lawyer, a doctor — all had failed, or had been ambitious for quicker betterment, and drifted to the golden land, there to feel the full weight of their own incompetence. They came there night after night, and when they had no money to gamble with they sauntered with the throng, or leaned heavily against the noble pillars which supported the ceiling. Thorpe afterward often wondered what had become of them. It is doubtful if there is a living soul who knows.

Occasionally Thorpe picked up a heap of

woman in the street, put it in a carriage, and saw it safely to a night's lodging. Sometimes the woman mumbled feeble gratitude, as often cursed him because he would not give her drink. One night, when rambling about alone, he knocked down a man who was beating a pretty young Mexican woman, then collared and carried him off to the calaboose. The girl died, and a few days later he went to the court-house to testify. The small room was packed; the jurors were huddled in a corner, where they not only listened to the testimony, but were obliged to talk out their verdict, there being no other accommodation.

The trial was raced through in San Francisco style, but lasted several hours. Thorpe sat it out. There was no testimony but his and that of the coroner; but the lawyer and the district-attorney tilted with animus and vehemence. When they had concluded, the judge rose, stretched himself, and turned to the jury.

"You 've heard the whole case," he remarked. "So you do you 're level best while I go out for a drink. He killed her or he did n't. It 's swing or quit." And, expectorating impatiently among the audience, he sauntered out.

The jury returned a verdict of "not guilty," and the man was lynched in the quiet and orderly manner of that time.

VII

A WEEK later forty or fifty people were camped beside the strawberry fields on the hills beyond the army posts and sloping to the ocean. Mr. Randolph and Nina, the McLanes, Miss Hathaway, Miss Shropshire, the "three Macs," the Earles, and a half-dozen young men were domiciled in a small village of tents on the eminence nearest the city. The encampments were a mile apart; and in the last of them a number of the Californian grandees who had made the land Arcadia under Mexican rule enjoyed the hospitality of Don Tiburcio Castro, a great rancher who was making an attempt to adapt himself to the new city and its enterprising promoters.

Thorpe and Hastings walked over from

the Presidio. They found the entire party assembled before the largest tent, which flew the American flag. As the young men approached, all of the ladies formed quickly into line, two and two, and walked forward to meet them. The men, much mystified, paused, raised their caps, and stood expectant. Mrs. McLane stepped from the ranks, and, with much ceremony, unrolled several yards of tissue paper, then shook forth the silken folds of the English flag, and presented it to Thorpe.

"It is made from our sashes, and we all sewed on it," she announced. "You will sleep better if the Union Jack is flying over your tent."

"How awfully jolly—what a stunning compliment," stammered Thorpe, embarrassed and pleased. "It shall decorate some part of my surroundings as long as I live."

Mr. Randolph himself fixed the flag, and Thorpe exclaimed impulsively to Mrs. McLane, with whom he stood apart: "Upon my word, I believe I am coming under the spell. I wonder if I shall ever want to leave California?"

"Why not stay? Unless you have ambitions, and want to run for Parliament or be a diplomat or something, or are wedded to the English on their native heath, I don't see why you should n't remain here. It is rather slow for us women: we are obliged to be twice as proper as the women of older civilisations; but a man, I should think, especially a man of resource like you, ought to find twenty different ways of amusing himself. You not only can have all that is exciting in San Francisco, watching a city trying to kick out of its long clothes, but you can saunter about the country and see the grandees in their towns and on their ranchos, to say nothing of the scenery, which is said to be magnificent."

"It is n't a bad idea. My past is not oppressing me, but I believe I should enjoy the sensation of beginning life over again. It would be that — certainly. But then I am an Englishman, you know, and English roots strike deep. Still, I have a half mind to buy a ranch here and come back every year or so. And I have a favourite brother who is rather delicate; it would be a good life for him."

"Do think of it," said Mrs. McLane, in the final tone with which she dismissed a subject that could claim her interest so long and no longer. She had liked Thorpe more in Paris, where he was not in love with another woman. She moved away with her husband, a big burly man with a face curiously like Sir Walter Scott's, and Thorpe plunged his hands in his pockets and strolled over the hill. The slopes were covered with strawberry vines down to the broad white beach. The large calm waves of the Pacific rolled ponderously in and fell down. Cityward was the Golden Gate with its white bar. Beyond it were steep cliffs, gorgeous with colour.

"Does England really exist?" he thought. "One could do anything reckless in this country."

He had been the only man to miss his elk at the hunt, and he had spent the rest of the day in hard riding. When the fever wore off, his reason was thankful that Nina Randolph had refused him, and he made up his mind to leave California by the next steamer. He had heard of the wonders worked by Time, and none knew better than he how to make life varied and interesting. He persuaded himself that he was profoundly relieved that she did not love him. Once or twice he had been nearly sure that she did. He had not seen her alone since the morning of the hunt, and, when they had met, her manner had been as frank and friendly as ever.

He joined Mrs. Earle, who had draped a reboso about her head, and was fluttering an immense fan. For the first time since his arrival in San Francisco, he plunged into a deliberate flirtation. Mrs. Earle was one of those women who flirt from the crown of her head to the sole of her foot, and she was so thin that Thorpe fancied he could see the springs which kept her skeleton in such violent motion. Her eyebrows were marvels of muscular ingenuity, and all the passions were in a pair of great black eyes which masked a brain too shrewd to try the indulgence of old Dom Pedro Earle, a doughty Scot, too far.

Once, as they repassed a tent, Thorpe saw a vibration of the door, and a half moment later heard a loud crash. Mrs. Earle's eyebrows went up to her hair, but she only said:

"Your eyes are as grey and cold as that sea, señor; but they will get into a fine blaze some day, and then they will burn a hole in some poor woman's heart. And your jaw! *Dios de mi alma!* What a tyrant you must be — over yourself most of all! I flirt with you no more. You are the sort of man that husbands are so jealous of, because you do not know how to trifle. *Adios, señor, adios!*"

She swayed over to her husband; and at the same moment Nina ran out of the tent which had attracted Thorpe's attention. She wore a short white frock and a large white hat, which made her look very young. In her hand she carried a small tin horn, upon which she immediately gave a shrill blast.

"That means work," she cried. "Get down to the patch."

The servants spread a long table on a level spot, and fetched water from a spring, carrying the jugs on their shoulders. The cook, in a tent apart, worked leisurely at a savory supper. The guests scattered among the strawberry-beds, and plucked the large red fruit. Each had a small Mexican basket, and culled as rapidly as possible; the, positions they were forced to assume were not comfortable. All were very gay, and now and then fought desperately for a well-favoured vine.

Nina, who had been ousted by Mrs. Earle's long arms, which flashed round a glowing patch like two serpents, sprang up and ran down to the foot of the hill, where the vines were more straggling and less popular. Thorpe followed, laughing. Her hat had been lost in the fray; her hair was down and blown about in the evening wind, and her cheeks were crimson.

"I hate long-legged long-armed giantesses," she exclaimed, attacking a vine spitefully. "And Spanish people are treacherous, anyhow. That patch was mine."

Thorpe laughed heartily. Her temper was genuine. His spirits suddenly felt lighter; she looked like a spoilt child, not like a girl with a tragic secret.

"She upset my basket, too," continued Nina, viciously. "But she upset half her own at the same time, and I trod on them on purpose."

"Here, let me fill your basket while you make a mud pie." He plucked his portion and hers, while she dug her fingers into the sand, and recovered her temper. As Thorpe dropped the replenished basket into her lap, she tossed her hair out of her eyes, and smiled up at him.

"Sit down and rest," she said, graciously. "Supper won't be ready for a half hour yet, and that hill is something to climb."

The others had finished their task, and disappeared over the brow of the hill. The west was golden; even the sea was yellow for the moment.

"We know how to enjoy ourselves out here," said Nina, contentedly, sinking her elbow into the sand. "I should think it a good place to pitch your tent."

She flirted her eyelashes at him, and looked so incapable of being serious that he answered, promptly, —

"I shall, if I can find some one to make it comfortable."

"You don't need to go begging. You 're quite the belle. Several that are more or less *éprises* are splendid housekeepers."

"I am not looking for a housekeeper."

"What are you looking for?" she asked, audaciously. Her chin was in her hand; her unbound hair clung about her; her tiny feet moved beneath the hem of her frock.

He also was lying on his elbow, his face close to hers. He had always followed her cues, and if she wished to flirt at this late date he was quite willing to respond. He made up his mind abruptly to dismiss all plans and drift with the tide.

"You," he said, softly.

"Are you proposing to me?"

He noted that she ignored his actual proposal, and commended her tact.

"I am not so sure that I am; I am surer that I want to."

"You are a cautious calculating Englishman."

"I believe I am — up to a certain point."

"Your face looks so hard and brown in that shadow. I 've had men propose the third time they met me."

"Probably."

"You can propose, if it will ease your mind. I shall never marry."

"Why not?"

"I think it would be heavenly to be an old maid, and make patchwork quilts for missionaries."

"I shall take pleasure in imagining you in the rôle when I am digging away at Blue Books and Reports."

"Ah, never, never more!" she chanted, lightly.

He paled slightly, then lifted a strand of her hair and drew it across his lips. It was the first caress he had given her in their six weeks of friendly intimacy, and her colour deepened. He shook the hair over her face. Her eyes peered out elfishly.

"I suspect we are going to flirt this week," she said, drily.

"If you choose to call it that." Her hair was clinging about his fingers.

"Suppose we make a compact — to regard nothing seriously that may occur this week."

"Why are you so afraid of compromising yourself?"

"That belongs to the final explanation. But it is a recognised canon of strawberry-week ethics that everybody flirts furiously.

Friendship is entirely too serious. Of course I shall flirt with you, — I shall let Dominga Earle see that at once, — as I am tired of all the others. Will you make the compact?"

"Yes."

The sun had dropped below the ocean; only a bar of paling green lay on the horizon. Voices came faintly over the hill, and the shadows were rapidly gathering.

Thorpe's face moved suddenly to hers. He flung her hair aside and kissed her. She did not respond, nor move. But when he kissed her again and again, she did not repulse him.

"I want you to understand this," he said, and his voice had softened, a rare variation, nor was it steady. "I have not let myself go because you proposed that compact. I am quite willing to forget it."

"But I am not. I expect you to remember it."

"Very well, we can settle that later. Meanwhile, for this week, we will be happy. Have you ever let any man kiss you before?"

"I don't know."

"You don't know? What a thing to say!"

"Some one may have found me napping, you know."

"You are very fond of being enigmatical. Why can't you give a straight answer to a straight question?"

"Well — what I meant was that you should not ask impertinent questions. But, if you insist, — as far as I know, only two men have kissed me, — you and my father."

He drew a quick breath. The ugliest fear that had haunted him took flight. He believed her to be truthful.

He stood up suddenly, and drawing her with him, held her closely until he felt her self-control giving way. When he kissed her again, she put up her arms and clung to him, and kissed him for the first time. He knew then, whatever her reason for suggesting such a compact, or her ultimate purpose, that she loved him.

The mighty blast of a horn echoed among the hills and cliffs. Nina sprang from Thorpe's arms.

"That is one of papa's jokes," she said. "It is n't the horn of the hunter, but of the farmer. Come, supper is ready. Oh, dear!" She clapped her hands to her head. "I can't go up with my hair looking like this. I can just see the polaric disgust of the Hathaway orbs; it goes through one like blue needles. And then the malicious snap of Mrs. Earle's, and the faint amusement of Mrs. McLane's. And I 've lost my hairpins! And I never—never—can get to my tent unseen. I 'm living with 'Lupie and Molly, and they 're sure to be late—on purpose; I hate women—Here! Braid it. Don't tell me you can't! You must!"

She presented her back to Thorpe, who was clumsily endeavouring to adapt himself to her mood. The discipline of the last six weeks stood him in good stead.

"Upon my word!" he exclaimed, in dismay, "I never braided a woman's hair in my life."

"Quick! Divide it in three strands—even—then one over the other— Oh, an idiot could braid hair! Tighter. Ow! Oh, you *are* so clumsy."

"I know it," humbly. "But it clings to my fingers. I believe you have it charged with electricity. It does n't look very even."

"I don't imagine it does. But it feels as if it would do. Half way down will be enough —"

"Hallo!" came Hastings's voice from the top of the hill. "Are you two lost in a quicksand?"

"Coming!" cried Nina. She sprang lightly up the hill, chattering as merrily as if she and the silent man beside her had spent the last half-hour flinging pebbles into the ocean.

They separated on the crest of the hill, and went to their respective tents. A few moments later Nina appeared at the supper-table with her disordered locks concealed by a network of sweet-brier. The effect was novel and bizarre, the delicate pink and green very becoming.

"Heaven knows when I 'll ever get it off," she whispered to Thorpe, as she took the chair at his side. "It has three thousand thorns."

The girls were in their highest spirit at the supper-table. Mr. McLane and Mr. Randolph were in their best vein, and Hastings and Molly Shropshire talked incessantly. Thorpe heard little that was said; he was consumed with the desire to be alone with Nina Randolph again.

But she would have no more of him that night. After supper, a huge bonfire was built on the edge of a jutting cliff, and the entire party sat about it and told yarns. The women stole away one by one. Nina was almost the first to leave.

The men remained until a late hour, and received calls from hilarious neighbours whose bonfires were also blazing. Don Tiburcio Castro dashed up at one o'clock, and invited Mr. Randolph to bring his party to a grand *merienda* on the last day but one of their week, and to a ball at the Mission Dolores on the evening following.

VIII

When the party broke up for the night Thorpe walked a half mile over the dunes, until, for any evidence of civilisation, he was alone in the wilderness, then lay down on the warm sand and took counsel with himself.

He had taken the plunge, and he had no regrets. He recalled his doubts, his certainty that the Randolph skeleton was not the figment of a girl's morbid imagination, his analysis of a temperament which he was only beginning to understand, and wherein lay gloomy foreshadowings, the fact that her first appeal had been to his animalism and that the appeal had been direct and powerful. Until the morning of the elk-hunt, he had not admitted that he loved her; but in a flash he had realised her tragic and desolate position, little as he guessed the cause, and coincidently his greater love for her had taken form so definitely that he had not hesitated a moment to ask her to marry him. Later, he had persuaded himself that he was well out of it; but between that time and this he had allowed himself hardly a moment for meditation.

To-night he had not a regret. The certainty that she loved him put his last scruple to flight, and changed his attitude to her irrevocably. He had never loved before, nor had she. She seemed indivisibly and eternally a part of him, and he recalled the sense of ownership he had experienced the night he had met her, when the evil alone in her claimed him. To-night the sense was stronger still, and he no longer believed that there was a spark of evil in her; the moment he became a lover, he became an idealist. He exaggerated every better quality into a perfection; and all other women seemed marionnettes beside the one who could make him shiver with hopes and fears, affect his appetite, and control his dreams, who made him wild to surrender his liberty before he was thirty, and accept a woman of the people as a mother-in-law.

The full knowledge suddenly poured into his brain that he was in love, he,—Dudley Thorpe, who had crammed his life so full of other interests that he had rarely thought of love, believing serenely that it would arrive when he was forty, and ready for it. He lay along the sands and surrendered himself to the experience, the most marvellous and delicious he had ever known. Once he caught himself up and laughed, then felt that he had committed a sacrilege. He knew that as he felt then, as he might continue to feel during his engagement, was an isolated experience in a man's life. He felt like clutching at even the tremours and fears that assailed him, and cutting them deep in his brain, that he might have their memory sharp and vivid when he was long married and serenely content. He was happier in those moments, lying alone on the dry warm sand under the crowding stars which had outlived so many passions, than when he had held her in his arms. He felt that something had escaped him when they had been together, some thought had strayed; and he determined to concentrate his faculties more fully and to become a master in love. He did nothing by halves, and he would be completely happy.

Then his thoughts became practical once more. Her admission that she loved him had given him a right to control her life, to protect her, to think for both. He was a very high-handed man, and, having made up his mind to marry Nina Randolph, he regarded her opposition as non-existent. He would argue it out with her, when she was ready to speak, knowing that the mental tide of woman, when undammed, must have its way; but he alone would decide the issue.

He should no longer torment himself with imaginings, rehearsing every ill that could befall a woman, whether the act of her own folly or the cruel hatching of Circumstance. It mattered nothing; he should marry her. His want of her was maddening. The desire to pluck her from her present life, to make her happy, possessed him.

IX

THE next morning all were up at eight and picking strawberries for breakfast. The prolonged and vociferous music of the horn had precluded all hope of laziness, and the late seekers after sleep were obliged to turn out with the best grace possible. A plunge in the sea had animated the men for the day, and the women were very fresh and amiable.

After breakfast they scattered about the hills and beach. It was a cloudless dark-blue day. The air was warm and dry. The bleak sand dunes were reclaimed for a brief season by the vivid green of willow and oak, the fields of purple lupin and yellow poppy; the trade winds were elsewhere, and the vegetation of San Francisco enjoyed its brief span of life. A ship with all her sails spread drifted, sleepily, over the bar.

Thorpe and Nina climbed an eminence from which they could see the Mission Dolores, far on the right, the smoke curling languidly from its great chimneys; the square Presidio of romantic memories and prosaic present; the distant city, whose loud feverish pulse they fancied they could hear.

They sat down under a tree. Nina took off her hat, and threw back her head. "I think I am the re-embodiment of some pagan ancestor," she said. "On days like this, I care nothing for a single responsibility in life, nor for what to-morrow will bring, nor for a religion nor a creed, nor for the least nor greatest that civilisation has accomplished. I don't even long for Europe and the higher intellectual life. It is enough that I am alive, that my eyes see only beauty, and my skin feels warmth. I worship the sun and the sky and the flowers and the trees and the sea, above all the warm quick atmosphere. They seem to me the only things worth loving."

"They are not the only things you love, however."

"No, I love you and my father. I hate my mother. But I always manage to forget her existence when I am off like this, and she is out of my sight —"

"Why do you hate your mother?"

"That is one of the things you are not to know yet. This week you are to hear nothing that is not pleasant. I wish you to feel like a pagan, too."

"I do. Some of your mandates are very easy to observe. We are reasonably sympathetic on more points than one."

"We will imagine that all life is to be like this week — only no allusion is to be made during this week to the future, and no allusion in the future to this week."

"I will do all I can to respect your wishes as to the first. The second is too ridiculous to notice. We will settle all that when the time comes."

To this she vouchsafed no reply, but peered up into the boughs. Her expression changed after a moment; it became impersonal, and her eyes hardened as they always did when her mind alone was at work.

"So far, California has evolved no literature," she said. "When it does, I don't doubt it will be a literature of light and charm and comedy — and pleasurable pathos. Writers will continue to go to the dreary moorlands, the dun-coloured skies of England for tragedy settings, and for the atmosphere of tradition and history. It will be hard for any writer who has travelled over the wonderful mountains and valleys of California — you have only seen the worst of it so far — to imagine tragedy in a land of such exultant beauty, under a sun that shines in a blue sky for eight months of the year. Fancy Emily Brontë writing 'Wuthering Heights' in California! The setting is all wrong for anything deeper than the picturesque crimes of desperadoes. But it is the very contrast, this very accompaniment of unreality, that makes our tragedies the harder to bear. I have thought sometimes that if I could come out here on a furious day in winter, and wander about the sand hills by myself, I'd feel as if I had a better right to be miserable —"

"I thought we were to have no more such hints this week. I am tired of innuendoes. As I have remarked before, you take an unfair advantage. Let down your hair. It looks full of gold and red in this light, and I want to see it spread out in the sun."

"Very well, put my hairpins in your pocket. Take it down yourself, and don't pull, on your life."

X

THE week passed very gaily; the mornings in long rambles, the early afternoon in siesta, its later hours in visits to neighbouring camps, followed by strawberry picking and long evenings about the fire or walking on the beach.

Thorpe and Nina were comparatively alone most of the time; and her high spirits, her lavish charm, her sudden moments of seriousness, and her outbursts of passionate affection completed his enthralment. Several times Thorpe caught Mr. Randolph's eyes following him with an expression of peculiar anxiety, and it chafed him not to be able to declare his purpose plainly; but for the week he was bound.

On the whole, it was a happy week. As it neared its end, Thorpe knew that his mind was possessing hers, that her will was weakening, and love flooding reason. Once or twice she gave him a glance of timid appeal; but she would not discuss the position. His mastery was the more nearly complete as he kept his promise and ignored the future.

On the last day but one the party went down the coast to attend Don Tiburcio's *merienda*. It was to be given in a valley about a half-mile inland, which the guests must approach through a narrow cañon fronting the sea.

The walk along the beach and inland trail was easy and pleasant, but the cañon was sown with rocks and sweet-brier; and the way was picked with some discomfort.

"If I stub my toe, you can carry me," said Nina.

"I will," said Thorpe, gallantly. He was feeling particularly light of heart. The week was almost over. Delightful in many ways as it had been, he was eager to take the reins into his own hands.

"Look! look!" exclaimed Nina, and the party paused simultaneously.

Don Tiburcio Castro had suddenly appeared at the head of the cañon. He was mounted on a large horse of a breed peculiar to the Californias, golden bronze in colour with silver mane and tail. The trappings of the horse were of embossed leather, heavily mounted with silver. His own attire was magnificent. He wore the costume of the grandees of his time, — a time which had fallen helplessly into the past during the fourteen years of American possession; indeed, Don Tiburcio, who, like many of his brethren, had for every day use adopted the garb of modern civilisation, had the effect, as he sat motionless on his burnished steed at the head of the cañon, of a symbolic figure at the end of a perspective.

He wore short clothes of red silk, the jacket open over a lace shirt clasped with jewels. His long botas of yellow leather were wound about with red and blue ribbons; his broad sombrero was heavy with silver eagles.

"I begin to feel the unreality of California," said Thorpe. "It is like a scene out of a picture-book."

"After all, it is but one phase," replied Nina.

Don Tiburcio lifted his sombrero and rode

down the cañon, the horse stepping daintily over the rocks. The women waved their handkerchiefs, the men their caps. Then the end of the perspective was closed once more, this time by a group of women. And they wore full flowered gowns with pointed bodice, rebosos draped about their dark graceful heads. Two tinkled the guitar. The others wielded large black fans.

"Ay!" exclaimed Mrs. Earle. "Why did I not bring my reboso? 'Lupie, we shall be forgotten."

"There are men," replied Miss Hathaway, as several dark beribboned heads appeared above the rebosos. "They, too, may want a change. You can desert me, Captain Hastings. I shall amuse myself."

"I don't doubt it," said Hastings, gloomily. "I don't flatter myself that I could make you jealous."

"I welcome you," said Don Tiburcio, choosing his English very slowly, and reining in. "The day ees yours, my friends. I am your slave. I have prepare a little entertainment, but if it no is to your taste, but say the word, and all shall be change."

Mr. Randolph made a terse and suitable reply. Don Tiburcio stood aside that all might pass him, bowing repeatedly; and the party made its way as quickly as possible to the entrance.

Doña Eustaquia Carillo de Brotherton, one of the most famous women of the old régime, stood there, the girls making way for her, and for Doña Jacoba Duncan, Mrs. Polk, — she who was beautiful Magdaléna Yorba, — and Doña Prudencia Iturbi y Moncada. The first was happy with her American husband; the second was not; Doña Jacoba's lines were as stern as when she had beaten her beloved children with a green hide reata, her smile as brilliant; and Doña Prudencia, who still (presumably) lamented the late Reinaldo, had found mitigation in her great social importance, and in her maternal devotion to the heir of her father-in-law's vast estates.

The women all kissed each other, and those that could talk Spanish made a soft pretty babel of sound that suggested perpetuity. The men were presented, and those of the Randolph party taken prompt possession of by the coquettish Californian girls. The men of the South were inclined to be haughty at first, but shortly succumbed to the novel charm of the American women.

"One can hardly realise the life they suggest," said Mr. Randolph to Thorpe. "Not fifty miles from San Francisco, they are still living in much of their primitive simplicity and state. In the south they are still farther removed from all that we have done. Doña Prudencia lives the life of a dowager empress."

They were in an open valley, shaded here and there with large oaks, carpeted with flowers. The women seated themselves on the warm dry ground, the caballeros, — as resplendent as Don Tiburcio, — and the more modest Americans lying at their feet, smoking the cigarito. The Californian girls tinkled their guitars and sang, with accompaniment of lash and brow. The older women smoked daintily, and talked of the gay old times. Thorpe, who was in no mood to parry coquetry, — and Nina was receiving the court of no less than three caballeros, — bestowed himself between Doña Eustaquia and Doña Prudencia, and charmed them with his unfeigned interest.

In the middle of the valley was a deep excavation. From stout poles hung two bullocks. In the course of an hour, the high beds of coals beneath the beasts were ignited, and the smell of roast meat mingled with the drowsy scent of the poppy and the salt of the sea.

When the bullocks were cooked, and the repast was spread some yards away, the guests found on the table every delicacy known to the old time. It was a very lively and a very picturesque feast, and no one felt the exhilaration of it more than Thorpe. He could not see Nina. She was on his side of the table, and eight or ten people were between; but it was enough to know that she was there, and that before the day was over they should find an hour together.

The wines until after the dessert were American; but as luncheon was concluding a servant brought a great tray covered with small glasses containing a colourless liquid.

"You must all dreenk with me to the glory and prosperity of California in my native wine, the fierce mescal," said Don Tiburcio, rising. "Every one — ah, yes, ladies, it ees strong:

I would not advise you that you take mooch; but one seep, just for the toast — ah, *muchas gracias.*"

The company rose. The American women made a doubtful little peck at the innocent-looking beverage, and shivered. The men consumed it heroically, repressing their tears. Thorpe felt as if he were swallowing live hornets; but, as he placed his glass on the table and bowed to the host, his face was quite stolid.

The company drove home, and retired at once to siesta. The strawberry picking was belated, and Nina gathered hers with the help of Mr. McLane. At dinner she sat between Mr. McLane and Hastings, and did not look at Thorpe. He racked his brain to remember what he could have done to offend her.

XI

They did not walk on the beach that evening, but sat about the fire, somewhat fatigued, but still in high spirits. Nina alone was quiet. After a time she stole away, and went down to the water. Thorpe was forced to infer that she wished to be alone, and did not follow her at once. When at the end of a half-hour she had not returned, his ill-carried impatience mastered him.

His feet made no sound on the sandy slope, nor on the beach. It was a night of perfect peace and calm and beauty. The ocean was quiet. The stars were thick; a thin young moon rode past them. But Nina was not within the flood of light about him. He turned the corner of a jutting rock, and came upon her.

She was sitting on a high stone, her hands pressed hard on her knees, staring out to sea. Thorpe had seen her face bitter, tragic, passionate; but he had never seen it look as it looked to-night. It might have been the face of a woman cast up by the ocean, out of its depths, or a face of stone for forty years. All the youth and life were out of it. It was fixed, awful. Thorpe stood appalled. The sweet intercourse of the past week seemed annihilated, the woman removed from him by a sudden breach in time, or some tremendous crash in Circumstance. He dared not speak, offer her sympathy. He felt that whether she had loved him or not in this hour of abandonment to her despair, he must be an insignificant feature in her life.

He stole away and sat down, dropping his face in his hands. His brain, usually clear and precise, whirled disobediently. He felt helpless, his manhood worthless. Nothing but a jut of rock stood between himself and Nina Randolph, and it might have been the grave of one of them. Chaos was in him, a troop of hideous imaginings. He wondered vaguely if the mescal had affected him. It was cursed stuff, and the blood had been in his head ever since he had drunk it.

He knelt down, and dashed the cold seawater over his face and head, not once, but several times. When he stood up, his brain was cool and steady.

"I must either go to her," he thought, "or despise myself. It is not an intrusion; I certainly have my rights."

He went rapidly round the bend, and lifted her from the stone before she was aware of his presence, then held her at arm's length, a hand on each shoulder.

The fixity left the muscles of her face. They relaxed in terror.

"What is your secret?" he demanded, peremptorily. "Have you had a lover — a child? Is that it?"

"No."

"On your word of honour?"

"Yes."

"Are your parents unmarried?"

"Not that I know of."

"Have you loved some man that is dead?"

"I have never loved any man but you."

"Have you committed a crime? Are you in constant terror of discovery?"

"I have never injured any one but myself."

"Is there insanity in the family, cancer, consumption?"

"No."

"Then, in God's name, what is it? I have the right to know, and I demand it; and the right to share your trouble and help you to bear it. I give you my word of honour that, no matter what it is, it shall make no difference to me."

She hung her head, and he felt her quiver from head to foot. Then she fell to weeping silently, without passion, but shaking painfully. He took her in his arms, and did what he could to comfort her, and he could be very tender when he chose. Later, he coaxed and implored and threatened, but she would not speak. Once she made as if to cling to him, then put her arms behind her and clasped her hands together. The act was significant; but Thorpe took no notice of it. He knew now that it was going to be more difficult to marry her than he had anticipated, that infinite tact and patience would be necessary. After a time, he dried her eyes and led her up the hill to the door of her tent. The others were still about the fire, and she went in unseen.

XII

Thorpe slept little that night. He wandered about the sand hills until nearly dawn. It seemed to him that he had exhausted the category of possible ills; he could think of nothing else. After all, it did not matter. The woman alone mattered. He knew that when he had persuaded her to marry him (he never used the word "if"), he could control her imagination and make her happy; and no other man alive could do it. In twenty different ways he could make her forget everything but the fact that she was his wife.

The next day Nina did not appear until the party was gathered about the table for luncheon. She explained that she had slept late in order to be in good trim for the party that night, and had spent the rest of the morning making an alteration in her evening frock.

She nodded gaily to Thorpe, and took a seat some distance from him. She looked very pretty. Her spirits, like her colour, were high, her eyes brilliant. Nevertheless, there was a change in her, indefinable at first; then Thorpe decided that she had acquired a shade of defiance, of hardness.

But he had no time for thought. Mrs. Earle's flashing eyes were challenging him on one side, Miss Hathaway's fathomless orbs on the other. Opposite, Miss Shropshire, for the first time, displayed an almost feverish desire to engage his attention, and made herself uncommonly agreeable.

The afternoon was spent in packing and resting for the dance. The only woman to be seen without the tents was Miss Shropshire, who took Thorpe for a long walk and entertained him with many anecdotes of Nina's eccentricities.

"She is very mutable," said Thorpe, at length; "but I should not have called her eccentric."

"Should not you?" demanded Miss Shropshire. "Now, I should. But then you have seen so much of the world, so many varieties of women. Nina seems very original to us out here. I often wonder, well as I know her, what she will say and do next. Oh, Mr. Thorpe, does not that ship look beautiful?"

But Thorpe, who found a certain satisfaction in talking of the beloved object, gently led her back to her former theme, and learned much of Nina's childhood and school-girl pranks. There was no hint of the mystery, nor did he wish that there should be.

Shortly after supper they started on horseback for the Mission, the evening gear following in a wagon. Horses and conveyance had been sent by Don Tiburcio.

Nina rode between Mr. McLane and Captain Hastings, and kept them laughing heartily. The day had passed and Thorpe had not had a word with her. He rode last, with Miss Hathaway, glad of her society; for she never expected a man to talk when he was not in the mood. Scarcely a word passed between them; once or twice he had an uncomfortable impression that her large cold inscrutable eyes were watching him intently.

They rode through the heavy dusk of a Californian night, perfume and the odd abrupt sounds of the New World about them. The landscape took new form in the shadows. The stunted brush seemed to crouch and quiver, ready to spring. The owl hooted across the sandy waste; and coyotes yapped dismally. Many of the party were silent; but Nina's fresh spontaneous laugh rang out every few moments, striking an incongruous note. California itself was a mystery in that hour and did not consort with the lighter mood of woman.

Suddenly they looked down upon the Mission. The church was dark, but the long wing beside it flared with light. They rode rapidly down the hill and across the valley. As they approached, they saw Don Tiburcio standing on the corridor before one of the open doors. He wore black silk short clothes and a lace shirt, his hair tied back with a ribbon. Diamonds blazed among his ruffles and on his long white hands.

As he was making one of his long and stately speeches, Miss Hathaway laid her hand on Thorpe's arm.

"Take my advice," she said, in her cool even tones. "Do not go near Nina to-night. Let her alone. I think she wishes it."

Thorpe made no reply. Miss Hathaway might as well have asked him to hold his breath until the entertainment was over.

The ladies went at once to a large room set aside for their use and donned their evening frocks. These frocks were very simple for the most part, organdie or swiss, and they were adjusted casually before the solitary mirror.

Nina's gown was of white nainsook ruffled to the waist with lace, and very full. The low cut bodice was gathered into the belt like a child's. Sometime since a local goldsmith of much cunning had, out of a bar of native gold, fashioned for her three flexible serpents. She wore one through her hair, one on her left arm, and a heavier one about her waist.

"*Dios de mi alma*, Nina," exclaimed Mrs. Earle; "you look like an imp to-night. What is the matter with you? Your eyes look — look — I hardly know what you do look like."

"Are you well, Nina?" asked Miss Hathaway, turning and smiting the girl with her polaric stare. "Have not you a headache? Why not lie down and not bother with this ball?"

For a moment Nina did not reply. She brought her small teeth together, and looked into Miss Hathaway's eyes with passionate resentment.

"Just mind your own business, will you?" she said, pitching her voice for the other woman's ear alone. "And you 'd oblige me by transfixing some one else for the rest of the evening. I 've had enough of your attentions for one day."

Then she shook out her skirts as only an angry woman can, and left the room.

"Nina is in one of her unpleasant moods to-night," said Mrs. McLane, attempting a glimpse of herself over Miss McDermott's shoulder, that she might adjust a hairpin.

"I have not seen her like this for some time — seven weeks," and she smiled.

"She looks like a little devil," said Mrs. Earle. "I have not been here long enough to become intimate with her moods, and I must say I prefer her without them. What are you scowling about, 'Lupie? Is your sash crooked? Can I fix it? But I forgot: you are above such trifles — Holy Mary! Guadalupe Hathaway! what on earth is the matter with your back?"

"What?" asked Miss Hathaway, presenting her back squarely. There was a simultaneous chorus of shrieks.

"Guadalupe, for Heaven's sake, what have you been doing?" cried Mrs. McLane. "Your back is striped — dark brown and white."

"Oh, is that all?" asked Miss Hathaway, gathering up her fan and gloves. "I suppose it got sunburned this morning at croquet. I had on a blouse with alternate thick and thin stripes. *Hasta luego!*" and she moved out, not with any marked grace, but with a certain dignity which saved the stripes from absurdity.

"*Bueno!*" exclaimed Mrs. Earle, "I'd like

to have as little vanity as that. How peaceful, and how cheap!"

"I suspect that it is her vanity to have no vanity," said Mrs. McLane, who was the wisest of women. "And if she did not happen to be a remarkably handsome girl, I fancy her vanity would take another form. But come, come, *mes enfants*, let us go. I feel half dressed; but as this is a picnic I suppose it does not matter."

The guests were assembled in the large hall of the Mission: Mr. Randolph's party, Don Tiburcio's, and several priests. The musicians were on the corridor beyond the open window. Doña Eustaquia, Doña Jacoba, Doña Prudencia, Mrs. Polk, and the priests sat on a dais at the end of the room; behind them was draped a large Mexican flag. The rest of the room was hung with the colours of the United States. The older women of the late régime wore the heavy red and yellow satins of their time, the younger flowered silks, their hair massed high and surmounted by a comb. The caballeros were attired like their host.

The guests were standing about in groups after the second waltz, when Don Tiburcio stepped to the middle of the room and raised his hand.

"My friends," he said, "my honoured compatriots, Don Hunt McLane and Don Jaime Randolph have request that we do have the contradanza. Therefore, if my honoured friends of America will but stand themselves against the wall, we of California will make the favourite dance of our country."

The Americans clapped their hands politely. Don Tiburcio walked up to Mrs. Earle, bowed low, and held out his hand. She rattled her fan in token of triumph over her Northern sisters, and undulated to the middle of the room her hand in her host's.

The swaying, writhing, gliding dance—the dance in which the backbone of men and women seems transformed into the flexible length of the serpent—was half over, the American men were standing on tiptoe, occasionally giving vent to their admiration, when Nina, her eyes sparkling with jealously and excitement, moved along the wall behind a group of people and stood beside Thorpe. He did not notice her approach. His hands were thrust into his pockets, his eyes eagerly fixed on the most graceful feminine convolutions he had ever seen.

"Dudley!" whispered Nina. He turned with a jump, and forgot the dancers.

"Well?" he whispered. "Nina! Nina!"

She slipped her hand into his. He held it in a hard grip, his eyes burning down into hers. "Why—why?—I must respect your moods if you wish to avoid me at times—but—"

"Do you admire that?"

"I did—a moment ago."

"Tell me how much."

"More than any dancing I have ever seen, I think," his eyes wandering back to the swaying colorous groups of dancers. "It is the perfection of grace—"

"Would you like to see something far, *far* more beautiful?"

"I fear I should go off my head—"

"Answer my question."

"I should."

"You say you respect my moods. I don't want—I particularly don't want to kiss you to-night. Will you promise not to kiss me if we should happen to be alone?"

Thorpe set his lips. He dropped her hand. "You are capricious—and unfair," he said; "I have not seen you alone for two days."

"It is not because I love you less," she said, softly. "Promise me."

"Very well."

"It is now ten. We shall have supper at twelve. At one, go down the corridor behind this line of rooms to the end. Wait there for me. Ask no questions, or I won't be there. This waltz is Captain Hastings'. I am engaged for every dance. *Au revoir.*"

Thorpe got through the intervening hours. He spent the greater part of them with the four doñas of the dais, and was warmly invited to visit them on their ranchos and in the old towns; and he accepted, although he knew as much of the weather of the coming month as of his future movements.

XIII

In the supper-room he sat far from Nina; but promptly at one he stole forth to the tryst. The windows looking upon the back corridor were closed. No one was moving among the mass of outbuildings. Not far away he could see the rolling surface and stark outlines of the Mission cemetery. A fine mist was flying before the stars; and a fierce wind, the first of the trades, was screaming in from the ocean.

Nina kept him waiting ten or fifteen minutes. Her white figure appeared at the end of the corridor and advanced rapidly. Thorpe met her half way, and she struck him lightly with her fan.

"Remember your promise," she said. "And also understand that you are not to move from the place where I put you until I give you permission. Do you take that in?"

"Yes," he said, sullenly; "but I am tired of farces and promises."

"Shh, don't be cross. This has been a charming evening. I won't have it spoiled."

"Are you quite well? Your colour is so high, and your eyes are unnaturally bright."

"Don't suggest that I am getting anything," she cried, in mock terror. "Small-pox? How dreadful! That is our little recreation, you know. When a San Franciscan has nothing else to do he goes off to the pest-house and has small-pox. But come, come."

He followed her into the room at the end of the corridor, and she lit a taper and conducted him up a steep flight of stairs which was little more than a ladder. At the top was a narrow door. It yielded to the knob, and Thorpe found himself in what was evidently the attic of the Mission.

"I was up here a month or two ago with the girls," said Nina. Her voice shook slightly. "I know there are candles somewhere — there were, at least. Stand where you are until I look."

She flitted about with the taper, a ghostly figure in the black mass of shadows; and in a few moments had thrust a half-dozen candles into the necks of empty bottles. These she lit and ordered Thorpe to range at intervals about the room. He saw that he was in a long low garret, at one end of which was a pile of boxes, at the other a heap of carpeting.

To the latter Nina pointed with her lighted taper. "Sit down there," she said, and disappeared behind the boxes.

Thorpe did as he was bidden. His hands shook a little as he adjusted the carpet to his comfort. The windows were closed. A tree scraped against the pane, jogged by the angry wind. The candles shed a fitful light, their flames bending between several draughts. The floor was thick with dust. Rafters yawned overhead, black and festooned with cobwebs. It was an uncanny place, and the sudden apparition of a large and whiskered rat scuttling across the floor in terrified anger at having his night's rest disturbed was not its most enlivening feature.

"Dudley!" said Nina, sharply.

"Yes?"

"Was that a rat?"

"It was."

"Oh, dear! dear! I never thought of rats. However," firmly, "I'm going to do it. I told you that you were not to move; but if you should happen to see a rat making for me, you go for him just as quickly as you can."

"The rats are much more afraid of you. The only danger you need worry about is pneumonia. I expect to sneeze throughout your entire performance — whatever it is to be."

"You press your finger on the bridge of

your nose: if you sneeze, it will spoil the effect of — of — a poem. Now, keep quiet."

For a moment he heard no further sound. Then something appealed to his ear which made him draw a quick breath. It was a low sweet vibrant humming, and the air, though unfamiliar, indicated what he had to expect. Sinking deeper into his dusty couch, he propped his chin on his hand; and, simultaneously, a vision emerged and filled the middle distance.

For a moment it stood motionless, poised, then floated lightly toward him, scarcely touching the floor, with a lazy rhythmic undulation which was music in itself. The full soft gown with its ruffles of lace rose and fell like billows of cloud, and in and out of a strip of crimson silk she twined and twisted herself to the slow scarce-audible vibration of her voice. She did not approach him closely, but danced in the middle and lower part of the room, sometimes in the full light of the candles, such as it was, at others retreating into the shadows beyond; where all outline was lost, and she looked like a waving line of mist, or a wraith writhing in an unwilling embrace.

And Thorpe? Outside, the storm howled about the corner of the Mission, or whistled a discord like a devil's chorus; but in the brain of the man was a hot mist, and it clouded his vision and played him many a trick. The dust of the floor, the grime of the walls, the unsightly rafters were gone. He lay on a couch as imponderable as ether. Overhead were strangely carven beams, barely visible in the dusk of the room's great arch. A gossamer veil of many tints, stirring faintly as if breathed upon, hung before walls of unimaginable beauty. The floor trembled and exhaled a delicious perfume. Flame sprang from opal bowls. But nothing was definite but the floating undulating shape which had wrought this enchantment. Its full voluptuous beauty, he recalled confusedly; dimmed by the shadows which clung to it even in the light, it looked vaporous, evanescent, the phantasm of a lorelei riding the sea-foam. Its swaying arms gleamed on the dark; the gold-scaled sea-serpents glided and twisted from elbow to wrist. Only the eyes were those of a woman, and they burned with a languid fire; but they never met his for a moment.

Suddenly, with abrupt transition, she changed the air, which had been almost a chant, and began dancing fast and furiously. Flinging aside the scarf, she clasped her hands under rigid arms, as if leaning on them the full weight of her tiny body. She danced with a headlong whirl that deprived her of her wraith-like appearance, but was no less graceful. With a motion so swift and light that her feet seemed continually twinkling in space, she sped up and down the garret like a mad thing; then, unlocking her hands, she flung them outward and spun from one end of the room to the other in a whirl so dizzy that she looked like a cloud blown before the wind, streaming with a woman's hair and cut with yellow lightning.

She flew directly up to where Thorpe lay, and paused abruptly before him. For the first time their eyes met. He forgot his promise. He stumbled to his feet, grasping at her gown even before he was risen. For a second she stood irresolute; then her supple body leaped backward, and a moment later had flashed down the room and through the door. Thorpe reached the door in three bounds. She was scrambling backward down the stair, her white frightened excited face dropping through the heavy dark. Thorpe got down as swiftly as he could; but she was far ahead, and he could not chase her into the Mission. When he re-entered the ball-room some time after, the guests were on the corridor waiting for their char-à-bancs. He returned to the Presidio in the ambulance.

XIV

The next day Thorpe called at the Randolphs'. The man, Cochrane, who, himself, looked yellow and haggard, informed him that the ladies were indisposed with severe colds. Thorpe went home and wrote Nina a letter, making no allusion to the performance at the Mission, but insisting that she recognise his rights, and let him know when he could see her and come to a definite understanding. A week passed without a reply. Then Thorpe, tormented by every doubt and fear which can assail a lover, called again. The ladies were still indisposed. It was Sunday. Thorpe demanded to see Mr. Randolph, and was shown into the library.

Mr. Randolph entered in a few moments, and did not greet Thorpe with his customary warmth. There were black circles about his eyes. His cheeks looked thinner and his hand trembled.

"Have you been ill, too?" asked Thorpe, wondering if South Park were a healthy locality.

"No; not ill. I have been much harassed — business."

"Nothing serious, I hope."

"It will right in time — but — in a new city — and with no telegraphic communication with the rest of the world — nor quick postal service — there is much to impede business and try the patience."

Thorpe was a man of quick intuitions. He knew that Mr. Randolph was lying. However, that was not his business. He rose and stood before the fire, nervously flicking his trousers with his riding-whip.

"Has it occurred to you that I love your

daughter?" he asked, abruptly. "Or — perhaps — she has told you?"

"She has not spoken to me on the subject; but I inferred as much."

"I wish, of course, to marry her. You know little about me. My bankers — and Hastings — will tell you that I am well able to take care of your daughter. In fact, I am a fairly rich man. This sort of thing has to be said, I suppose — "

"I have not misunderstood your motives. I misjudge few men; I have lived here too long."

"Oh — thanks. Then you have no objection to raise?"

"No; I have none."

"Your daughter loves me." Thorpe had detected a slight accent on the pronoun.

"I am sure of that."

"Do you mean that Mrs. Randolph might object?"

"She would not be consulted."

Thorpe shifted his position uneasily. The hardest part was to come.

"Nina has intimated to me," he said, haltingly, "that there is a — some mysterious reason which would prevent her marrying. I have utterly disregarded that reason, and shall continue to do so. I purpose to marry her, and I hope you will — will you? — help me."

Mr. Randolph leaned forward and twisted his nervous pale hands together. It was at least three minutes before he spoke, and by that time Thorpe's ear-drums were pounding.

"I must leave it to her," he said, "utterly to her. That is a question which only she can decide — and you. Of course she will tell you — she is too honest not to; but I am afraid she will stave it off as long as possible. I cannot tell you; it would not be just to her."

"But you will do nothing to dissuade her?"

"No; she is old enough to judge for herself. And if she decides in your favour, and you — are still of the same mind, I do not deny that I shall be very glad. I should even be willing for you to take her to England, to resign myself never to see her again — if I could think — if you thought it was for the best."

"I wish I knew what this cursed secret was," said Thorpe, passionately. "I am half distracted with it."

"Have you no suspicion?"

"It seems to me that I have thought of everything under heaven; and she denied one question after the other. I am bound to take her word, and to believe that the truth was the one thing I did not hit upon."

"Yes; if you had guessed, I think she would have told you, whether she was ready or not. It is very strange. You are one of the sharpest men I have ever met. Still, it is often the way."

"When can I see Nina?"

"In a few days—a week, I should say. Her cold is very severe."

"I have written to her, and she has not answered. Is it possible that her illness is serious? I have put it down to caprice or some new qualm."

"There is no cause for alarm. But she has some fever, and pain in her eyes, and is irritable. When she is well I will take it upon myself to see that you have an interview."

"Thank you." Mr. Randolph had not risen, but Thorpe felt himself dismissed. He left the house in a worse humour than he had entered it. He felt balked, repulsed, and disagreeably prescient. For the first time in his life, he uneasily admitted that an iron will alone would not keep a man on the straight line of march to his goal, that there was a chain called Circumstance, and that it was forged of many metals.

XV

THORPE determined not to go to the house again until either Nina or Mr. Randolph sent for him. He would not run after any woman, he told himself angrily; and once or twice he was in a humour to snap the affair in two where it was and leave the country. But, on the whole, the separation whetted his passion. That airy fabric of sentiment, imagination, and civilisation called spiritual affinity, occasionally dominated him, but not for long. His last experience of her had gone to his head: it was rarely that of all the Nina Randolphs he knew he could conjure any but the one that had danced his promise out of memory. There were times when he hated himself and hated her. Then he told himself that this phase was inevitable, and that later on, when the better part of their natures were free to assert themselves, they would find each other.

A week after his interview with Mr. Randolph, he found himself in South Park a little after eleven at night. He had dined on Rincon Hill, and purposed spending the night at the Oriental Hotel; he rarely returned to the Presidio after an evening's entertainment.

He had avoided the other men, and started to walk into town. Almost mechanically he turned into South Park, and halted before the tall silent house which seemed such a contemptible barrier between himself and the woman he wanted. His eyes, travelling downward, noted that a basement window had been carelessly left open. He could enter the house without let — and the opportunity availed him nothing. He wished that he were a savage, with the traditions and conventions of a savage, and that the woman he loved dwelt in a tent on the plain.

Lights glimmered here and there in the houses of South Park, but the Randolphs' was blank; everybody, apparently, was at rest. To stand there and gaze at her window was bootless; and he cursed himself for a sentimental ass.

He walked up the semi-circle and returned. This time he moved suddenly forward, lifting his head. It seemed to him that a sound—an odd sound—came from the bedroom above the parlour, a room he knew to be Mrs. Randolph's.

At first the sound, owing to the superior masonry of the walls, was muffled; but, gradually, Thorpe's hearing, naturally acute, and abnormally sensitive at the moment, distinguished the oral evidence of a scuffle, then the half-stifled notes of angry and excited voices. He listened a moment longer. The sounds increased in volume. There was a sudden sharp note, quickly hushed. Thorpe hesitated no longer. If the house of a man whose guest he had been were invaded by thieves, and perhaps murderers, it was clearly his duty to render assistance, apart from more personal reasons.

He took out his pistol, cocked it, then vaulted through the window, and groping his way to a door opened it and found himself in the kitchen entry. A taper burned in a cup of oil; and guided by the feeble light he ran rapidly up the stair.

He opened the door at the head, paused a a moment and listened intently. The house teemed with muffled sounds; but they fell from above, and through closed doors, and from one room. Suddenly the hand that held the pistol fell to his side. The colour dropped from his face, and he drew back. Was he close upon the Randolph skeleton? Had he not better steal out as he had come, refusing to consider what the strange sounds proceeding from the room of that strange woman might mean? There were no signs of burglars anywhere. A taper burned in this hall, likewise, and on the table beside it was a gold card-receiver. There had been a heavy rainfall during the evening, but there was no trace of muddy boots on the red velvet carpet.

Then, as he hesitated, there rang out a shriek, so loud, so piercing, so furious, that

Thorpe, animated only by the instinct to give help where help was wanted, dashed down the hall and up the stair three steps at a time. Before he reached the top, there was another shriek, this time abrupt, as if cut short by a man's hand. He reached Mrs. Randolph's room and flung open the door. But he did not cross the threshold.

The room flared with light. The bedding was torn into strips and scattered about. Every fragile thing the room contained was in ruins and littered the carpet. And in their midst, held down by Mr. Randolph and his servant, Cochrane, was a struggling, gurgling, biting thing which Thorpe guessed rather than knew was the mother of Nina Randolph. Her weak evil face was swollen and purple, its brutality, so decently cloaked in normal conditions, bulging from every muscle. Her ragged hair hung in scant locks about her protruding eyes. Over her mouth was the broad hand of the man, Cochrane. Mrs. Rinehardt, her face flushed and her dress in disorder, stood by the mantel crying and wringing her hands.

Thorpe's brain received the picture in one

enduring flash. He was dimly conscious of a cry from unseen lips, and the vanishing train of a woman's gown. And then Mr. Randolph looked up. He relaxed his hold and got to his feet. His face was ghastly, and covered with great globes of sweat.

"Thorpe!" he gasped. "You! Oh, go! go!"

Thorpe closed the door, his fascinated gaze returning for a second to the Thing on the floor. It no longer struggled. It had become suddenly quiet, and was laughing and muttering to itself.

He left the house, and walked out of the park and city, and toward the Presidio. It was a long walk, over sand drifts and rocks, and through thickets whose paths he had forgotten. The cold stars gave little light, for the wind drove a wrack aslant them; and when the colder dawn came, greying everything, the flowers that looked so brilliant in the sunlight, the heavy drooping trees, the sky above, he found himself climbing a high sand hill, with no apparent purpose but to get to the top; a cut about its base would have shortened the journey. He reached the summit, and saw the grey swinging ocean, the brown forts in their last sleep.

He sat down, and traced figures on the sand with his stick. Chaos had been in him; but the tide had fallen, and his thoughts were shaping themselves coherently. Nina Randolph was the daughter of a madwoman, and the seeds were in her. Her strange moods, her tragic despair, her hints of an approaching fate, her attitude to himself, were legible at last. And Miss Hathaway knew, and had tried to warn him. Doubtless others knew, but the secret had been well kept.

He was filled with bitterness and dull disgust, and his heart and brain were leaden. The mad are loathsome things; and the vision of Nina, foaming and hideous and shrieking, rose again and again.

That passed; but he saw her without illusion, without idealisation. She had been the one woman whose faults were entrancing, whose genuine temperament would have atoned for as many more. She seemed now a very ordinary, bright, moody, erratic, seductive young person who was making the most of life before she disappeared into a padded cell. He wondered why he had not preferred Miss Hathaway, or Mrs. Earle, or Miss McDermott. He had not, and concluded that her first influence had been her only one, and that his imagination had done the rest.

The sunrise gun boomed from the Presidio. The colours of dawn were on horizon and water. He rose and walked rapidly over the hills and levels; and when he reached his room, he went to bed and slept.

XVI

At two o'clock, just after Thorpe had breakfasted, Mr. Randolph's card was brought to him, and he went at once into the general sitting-room. No one but Mr. Randolph occupied it at the moment. He was sitting listlessly on the edge of a chair, staring out of the window. Commonly the triggest of men, his face to-day was unshaven, and he looked as if he had not been out of his clothes for forty-eight hours. And he looked as if he had been picked up in the arms of Time, and flung across the unseen gulf into the greyness and feebleness of age.

As he rose mechanically, Thorpe took his hand in a strong clasp, forgetting himself for the moment.

Mr. Randolph did not return the pressure. He withdrew his hand hurriedly, and sat down.

"An explanation is due you," he said, and even his voice was changed. "You have stumbled upon an unhappy family secret."

Thorpe explained how he had come to enter the house.

"I supposed that it was something of the sort, or rather Cochrane did; he found the window and lower door open. It was a kind and friendly act. I appreciate the motive." He paused a moment, then went on, "As I said just now, an explanation is due you, if explanation is necessary. As you know, I had recognised that as Nina's right — to speak when she saw fit. That is the reason I did not explain the other day — I usually manage to have her in the country at such times," he added, irrelevantly.

"Such attacks are always more or less unexpected, I suppose." Thorpe hardly knew what to say.

Mr. Randolph fumbled at his hat, "More or less."

"Were any other members of her family — similarly afflicted?"

"Her father and mother were well-conducted people. I know nothing of any further antecedents."

"It sometimes skips a generation," said Thorpe, musingly.

Mr. Randolph brought his hand close above his eyes, and pressed his lips together. He opened his mouth twice, as if to speak, before he articulated, "Sometimes, not always."

Thorpe rose abruptly and walked to the window, then returned, and stood before Mr. Randolph.

"And Nina?" he demanded, peremptorily. "What of her?"

Mr. Randolph pressed his hand convulsively against his face.

Thorpe turned white; his knees shook. He went out and returned with some brandy. "Here," he said. "Let us drink this and brace up and have it out. We are not children."

Mr. Randolph drank the brandy. Then he replied, "She is on the way. In a few years she will be as you saw her mother last night; no power on earth can save her. I would give my wretched failure of a life, I would burn at the stake—but I can do nothing."

"Perhaps I can. I intend to marry her."

"No! No! She, who is stronger than I, would never have permitted it. She told me that this morning. For the matter of that I am her ambassador to-day. She charged me to make it clear to you that she expected you to stand by your part of the compact. She is immovable; I know her."

"Tell her that I will take no messages at second hand, not even from you. Unless she sees and comes to an understanding with me, I shall consider myself engaged to her, and shall announce it."

"Do you mean to say that you would marry her, knowing what you do?"

"I would rather I had known it when I first came. I should have avoided her, or left the place. But I gave her my word, voluntarily, that nothing, no matter what, should interfere with my determination to marry her, and nothing shall."

"You *are* an Englishman!" said Mr. Randolph, bitterly. "I wish I were as good a one; but I am not. My record is clean enough, I suppose; but I am a weak man in some respects, and I started out al. wrong. I wish to God that everything were straight, Thorpe; I would rather you married her than any man I have ever known."

"Thank you. Will you arrange an interview for me?"

Mr. Randolph fidgeted, "I tell you what I think, Thorpe; you had better wait a little. She is in no mood to listen to reason, nor for love-making — take my word for that. I have never seen her in so black a mood. But women are naturally buoyant, and she particularly so. Go and take your trip through the State. Let it last — say two months, and then appear unexpectedly at Redwoods. I do not give you any encouragement, — in all conscience you ought not to want any; but I think that under the circumstances I suggest your final interview will at least not be an unpleasant one. Nina lives an out of door life there and is with the other girls most of the time."

"Very well. I don't know but that I prefer it that way. Meanwhile, will you tell her all that I have said? — except that I would rather I had known it sooner."

Mr. Randolph rose and gathered up his hat and gloves. "I will tell her," he said. "Good-bye. You are badly broken up, but you may be thankful that you are in your shoes, not mine."

XVII

Doña Prudencia had sent Thorpe a pressing invitation to be a guest at Casa Grande during the festivities celebrating the nineteenth birthday of her son. The day after his interview with Mr. Randolph, in company with Don Tiburcio Castro, Captain Brotherton and his wife, Doña Eustaquia, Mrs. Polk, and a half-dozen other native Californians, he took passage on a steamboat bound for Santa Barbara. The journey lasted four days, and was very uncomfortable; but the happy careless Spanish people were always entertaining, and the girls demanded the constant attentions of the Englishman. Thorpe had little time for thought and wished for none. When not playing squire to the women, he listened to Don Tiburcio's anecdotes of Old California, or discussed the future of the territory with Captain Brotherton, who was living a life of peace and plenty on a rancho, but nevertheless took an unfailing interest in the country his gallantry had helped to capture and hold.

The ship rode to anchor in the Santa Barbara channel before an animated scene. The adobe walls of Casa Grande had a new coat of white, the tiles a new coat of red; so had the great towers and arches and roof of the Mission, jutting before the green of its hills, a mile beyond. The houses about the fort looked fresh and gay. Many horses, richly caparisoned, pranced in the open court of Casa Grande, or pawed the ground by neighbouring trees. Caballeros, in their rich native costumes, were sauntering about, smoking cigaritos. On the corridors of the great and lesser houses were the women, brilliantly dressed, their heads draped with the reboso or mantilla, manipulating the inevitable fan.

Indians in bright calico garments stood on the beach, awaiting the luggage of the guests. Between them and the houses was a large booth, defiantly flaunting the colours of Mexico. Far to the left was a rude street, flanked on either side by a row of cheap wooden houses, the ugly beginning of an American town.

"It is all like a scene out of a picture-book," said Thorpe. "Can San Francisco — awful San Francisco! — be in the same territory? It looks like Arcadia."

"Si, is pretty," said Mrs. Polk, with a pensive sigh. "But no all the same like before, señor. Not the same spirit, for all know that their country is gone for ever, and that by and by the Americanos live in all the towns, so that the Spanish towns will be no more — and in a few years. But they like to meet and try to think is the same, and forget."

The passengers were landed in boats. The young heir, a tall lad with a handsome indolent face, and a half-dozen of his guests, came down to the shore to welcome the newcomers.

"Very good look, that boy," said Doña Eustaquia. "I not have seen him for some years, so uncomfortable this treep. But he have the face weak, like the father. Never I like Reinaldo Iturbi y Moncada; but I wish he not have been kill by Diego Estenega. Then, how different is California!"

As the boat touched the sands young Reinaldo came forward with a charming grace to help the ladies to land, and was kissed by each, with effusion. Indeed, there was so much kissing, and such an immediate high shrill chattering, such a profusion of "*queridas*," and "*mijitas*," and "*mi amigas*," that Thorpe, after exchanging a few words with his host, made haste to the house.

Doña Prudencia, clad in the richest of black satins, with a train a yard long and a comb six inches high, came forward to the edge of the corridor to greet him. She looked very pretty and plump and consequential.

"So good you are to come, Señor Torp," she said softly, giving him her little hand with a gesture which drew down his lips at once.

"I shall never forget how good you have been to ask me," he said, enthusiastically. "This picture alone was worth coming to California for."

"Ay! You shall see more than theese, Señor Torp. It ees an honour to receive you in the *casa* of the Iturbi y Moncadas. It ees yours, señor, burn it if you will. Command my servants like they are your own."

Thorpe, by this time, knew something of the peculiar phrasing of native Californian hospitality, and merely bowed and murmured acknowledgments.

The other guests came up at the moment, and there was another Spanish chorus, an agitated wave along the three-sided corridor. Thorpe glanced curiously about him. The black-eyed women were undulating and coquetting for the benefit of the new men, while throwing kisses and rapturous exclamations to Doña Eustaquia and the girls in her charge. Thorpe looked over more than one big fan. Suddenly his attention was attracted by a woman on the opposite corridor. She had risen, and was looking intently at Doña Eustaquia, who as yet had not glanced across the court. She was a very beautiful woman, the most beautiful woman Thorpe had seen in California, and her face was vaguely familiar. She looked very Spanish, but her hair was gold and her eyes were as green as the spring foliage. Then there was a sharp feminine shriek behind him; he was thrust aside, and Doña Eustaquia ran past him, crying, "Chonita! Chonita!" The beautiful stranger met her half way, and they embraced and kissed each other on either cheek some fifteen times.

"Que! Que! Que!" the women of his party were exclaiming, and then followed a deluge of words of which he could separate only "Chonita Estenega." They, in turn, ran forward, and were received with a manner so polished that it was almost cold. Thorpe had recognised her. He had met her at a court ball in Austria, where, as the wife of the Mexican minister, she had been the most admired woman in the palace.

"Is Don Diego Estenega here?" he asked Prudencia. "I met him a number of times in Vienna, and should like to meet him again."

Prudencia drew up her small important person with an expression of conscious virtue that did not confine itself to her face, but made her very gown swell and rustle.

"Si!" she said. "He ees here — for the firs' time in mos' twenty years, señor. You never hear? He killing my husban'. But I forgive him because ees in the fight and no can help. Reinaldo attack, and Diego mus' defend, of course. Still, he *kill* him, and I am the wife. But bime by I forgive, for that ees my religion. And I love Chonita. So she come to the old house, the firs' time in so many years, for the birfday de my son. Diego is horseback now, but come back soon. You no like go to your room? So dirt that treep, no? Reinaldo!" Her son came forward at once. "Show the Señor Torp to his room, no? and the other gentlemens."

Thorpe followed young Iturbi y Moncada down the corridor and into a small room. The floor was bare, the furniture prison-like; but he had heard of the simplicity of the adobe mansions of Californian grandees.

Reinaldo jerked open the upper drawer of the bureau, disclosing several rows of large goldpieces.

"At your service, señor," he said with a bow. "I beg that you will use it all."

Thorpe reddened to his hair. He hardly knew whether to be angry or not. Did these haughty grandees take him for a pauper? However, he merely bowed and thanked the youth somewhat drily, and at the same moment Captain Brotherton entered the room.

"The hospitality of the Californian!" he cried, taking in the situation at a glance. "Reinaldo, I see the new generation has forgotten nothing, despite the Americans."

"No, señor," said the young man, proudly. "What ours is, is our guests. That is right always, no? But perhaps the gentleman no like, perhaps he no have the custom in his country."

"We have not, I regret to say, Don

Reinaldo. We are a tight-fisted practical race. But I can the more deeply appreciate your hospitality; and, believe me, I do appreciate it."

"And you will use it — all, señor?"

Thorpe hesitated the fraction of a moment, then replied with some difficulty, "Certainly, señor. I will use it with the greatest pleasure."

"Many thanks, señor. *Hasta luego!*" And he left the room.

"What an extraordinary custom!" exclaimed Thorpe. "I can't use that man's money."

"Oh, you must! He 'd be terribly cut up if you did not — think you flouted him."

"Well, I 'll gamble with him, and let him win it back. I suppose he gambles."

"Rather. Before he is forty the Americans will have had his last acre, and he inherits four hundred thousand. They have not even the soil in which to plant a business instinct, these Californians. I am glad you have come in time. They are worth seeing, and their like will never be seen again."

"I should think they were worth seeing.

What did Doña Prudencia mean by saying that Diego Estenega killed her husband?"

"There was a fight to the death between them, and it was one or the other. Chonita, to the surprise of everybody, and to the horror of some — including the clergy — married Estenega at once, and went with him to Mexico. The old gentleman was in a towering rage, but forgave them later and visited them several times. He had large sums of money invested in Mexico which he left to Chonita. His Californian estates he left to young Reinaldo, whom he idolised. Estenega had had great hopes and plans in connection with this country which were dashed by Iturbi y Moncada's death. However, it was as well, for he is now one of the wealthiest and most powerful men in the Mexican government, and has been ambassador or minister abroad several times. But my wife will tell you the whole story when you come to visit us. Perhaps she will read it to you, for she has made a novel out of it, which may or may not be published after the death of all concerned. Here is your trunk. I'll leave you to clean up."

XVIII

Thorpe dressed for dinner, pocketed a roll of the gold with a wry face, and went to the *sala*, a long room opening on the middle corridor. Prudencia, in a red-satin gown, so thick that it stood out about her as if hooped, and flashing jewels on a great deal of white skin, her hair piled high and surmounted with a diamond comb, sat in the middle of the room talking volubly to her sister-in-law, who stood by the mantel looking sadly about her. Chonita had lost little of her beauty. She had had but two children; and vanity had kept the lines of her figure, the gliding grace of her walk, unchanged. She had known, during the twenty years of her married life, the great joys and the great disappointments, the exaltation and the terrified recognition of mortal weakness and limitations, inseparable to two such natures. But, on the whole, she was happy, and she and her husband were very nearly one.

"No, no, my Chonita!" Prudencia was exclaiming in her own tongue. "Why shouldst thou be sad? It is nearly twenty years; one cannot remember so long. Thou hast thine own house, far more elegant than this, I am told: why shouldst thou feel sad to come back? Thou art wealthy, and hast a devoted husband,—*ay de mi*, my Reinaldo! (but I could have had others),—and art as beautiful as ever, although I do not agree with some that thou hast not grown a day older. Thou hast the expression of years, if not its lines and grey hairs. I need not have grown stout; but I have no vanity, and walking is such trouble, and I love *dulces*. Besides, we do not carry our flesh into the next world; so Reinaldo, who hated fat women— Ay, Señor Torp, pardon me, no? I not did see you. I wish mooch to present you to my sister-in-law—Doña Chonita Iturb y Moncada de Estenega, Señor Torp of Eengland, *mijita*."

Çhonita came forward and held out her hand, smiling. "I remember meeting you in Austria," she said. "It was so warm that night in the palace, I remember, it made me talk of California to you. My husband is very glad to think that he shall meet you again."

"I am glad you come to cheer her up, Señor Torp," said Prudencia. "She feel blue because coming to the old house once more."

Thorpe looked at Chonita with the quick sympathy of the Englishman for terra ego, and Chonita flashed her acknowledgment. "Yes, I am a little sad," she said; "not only because it is the first time in so many years, but because it is probably for the last time in my life. My husband does not care for California. Here he is."

Estenega entered with several other men, and, recognising Thorpe at once, greeted him with a warmth that was more cosmopolitan than Californian, but none the less sincere. He showed the wear and tear of years. Ambitions, scheming, hard work had left their furrows, and the grey was in his hair. But his nervous vitality was undiminished, and his air of command even more pronounced than in the old days. He carried Thorpe off to discuss the growing complications between the North and South; and the conversation was resumed after dinner, despite the attractions of the *sala;* for news of the great world came infrequently to California, and the stranger who had recently lived in the midst of affairs was a welcome acquisition. Thorpe spent the greater part of the night in the billiard-room with Reinaldo, and got rid of his gold.

XIX

At sunrise he was awakened by the booming of cannon and the ringing of bells. He sprang out of bed, thinking that the United States was firing on the Mexican flag, then remembered that it was the birthday of the young heir, and turned in again.

Two hours later, he was shaken out of his morning nap by Estenega.

"How would you like a dip before breakfast? They are all up at mass, and Brotherton and I are going down to a very good cove I know of."

"Get out, and I'll be with you in ten minutes."

Santa Barbara looked like a necropolis when he emerged. Every soul in the town, with the exception of himself, Estenega, Brotherton, and the servants preparing the birthday breakfast, was on his knees in the Mission mumbling aves for young Reinaldo. The three men walked down to the bright-blue channel motionless under a bright-blue sky. The air was warm; the waves were warm; the fruit was ripening on the walls. The poppies were opening their deep yellow lips, breathing forth the languor of the land. The palms were tall and green. The spiked cactus had burst into blood-red flower.

"This is not America," said Thorpe. "It is Italy or Spain or Greece. It is another atmosphere, physical as well as mental. One could lie on the sands all day and think of nothing."

"California has a physical quality which the Americans and all the other races that will eventually pour into her can never change," said Estenega. "She will never cease to protest that she was made for love and wine and to enfold with content in the mere fact of existence, to delight the eye, the soul, and the body, to inspire poetry and romance, and that the introduction of the commercial element is an indignity. I used to think differently when California and my own ambitions seemed identical; but San Francisco gave me a nightmare."

"On the ranchos it is much the same as ever," said Captain Brotherton, "and will remain so long beyond our time. You will return with us, Mr. Thorpe? Estenega and Chonita go too."

And Thorpe gratefully accepted.

As they returned, they saw the great company streaming down from the Mission, a mass of colour. Few were on foot. No Californian walked a mile, if he had a horse to ride.

Thorpe hastened to his room to make his morning toilet. When he left it, the court and corridors were crowded with the brilliantly plumaged men and women. Reinaldo, in blue silk, was strutting about among the girls, as proud and happy as a girl dressed for her first party. There was no question in his mind who was the most important young man in California that morning. He was the head and front of California's wealthiest and haughtiest family, the scion of the only aristocracy that great territory would ever know. The Americans he regarded as a mere incident, — a brusque unpolished breed whose existence he rarely recalled. The Jews, up in the town, he considered with more favour; his fond mamma was inclined to be close-fisted with growing sons.

The tables had been set about the three corridors, as not only the neighbours were bidden to the breakfast, but many from distant ranchos. The poor were fed in the open beyond, on pigs roasted whole, and many dulces. The Presidio band played the patriotic and sentimental airs of Mexico.

Thorpe sat between Prudencia (who appeared to have marked him for her own) and Doña Eustaquia. Chonita was opposite, between two of her old admirers.

"It is the same, yet not the same — like the old time," said Doña Eustaquia, with a sigh.

"It is not the same at all," said Chonita. "It is a theatre, and we are performing — for Mr. Thorpe's benefit."

"No is theatre at all," said Prudencia, disapprovingly. "All is exactamente the same. Few years older, no more; but no one detail differente. And next year the same, and every year, — one, two, three hundred years what coming."

Chonita shrugged her shoulders, and did not condescend to answer, although every Californian within earshot, except Doña Eustaquia, assured her that Prudencia was right.

To Thorpe, who had no fond reminiscences, it all seemed natural and surpassingly picturesque. The highly seasoned dishes held hot controversy with his English stomach; and he found it hard to catch the meaning of the pretty broken-English wafted to him from prettier lips; but he was deeply thankful that for the moment his personal life could have no voice in so incongruous a setting.

After breakfast, the party went at once to a large arena near the pleasure-grounds of Casa Grande, and sat upon the raised seats about the ring, while Reinaldo and other young caballeros exhibited their skill and prowess against the pugnacious bull.

After siesta the people danced their national jigs in the court of Casa Grande, while the men and women of the aristocracy lounged over the railing of the corridors and encouraged them with handfuls of silver coins.

Thorpe, Estenega, and Captain Brotherton, in the ugly garb of a wider civilisation, stood apart.

"They are an anachronism," said the Englishman, "and will never be able to hold their own, namely, their vast possessions, against the sharp-witted American."

"Not ten years," said Estenega. "The sharpers are crouching like buzzards on the edge of every town. Up there in the village they have wares to tempt the Californians,—fashions and ornaments that cannot be bought otherwise without a trip to San Francisco. As there is little ready money, the Californians—who make their purchases by the wholesale, and would disdain to buy less than a 'piece' of silk or satin—mortgage small ranchos at an incredible rate of interest, against the next hide yield. Then the squatters have come, imperturbable and patient, knowing that when their case is tried, it will be before an American judge. When my father-in-law asked me whether I would prefer at his death his Mexican investments or half of his Californian leagues, I chose the former unhesitatingly: although he reckoned his landed estates at twice the value of the other. But I had no wish to come back here to live, and could trust no one else to look after my interests. Eustaquia is all right, for she has Brotherton. I notice the Californian women are marrying Americans wherever they can."

"And the matches are rather successful," said Brotherton, laughing. "Unfortunately, the American girls won't marry Californians, or the problem would be easily solved."

The day finished with a dance in the sala; and later, in Reinaldo's room, Thorpe lost the last of his host's gold and a roll of his own. The game was monté, and the young Californians grew so excited that Thorpe momentarily expected to see the flash of knives. They shouted and swore; and Reinaldo even wept with rage, and vowed that Thorpe was his only friend on earth.

However, the night ended peacefully. When the young men had become so laden with mescal that they could no longer see their cards, they embraced affectionately and went to bed.

XX

The next day there were races, and in the evening another dance, on the day following a *rodeo* and *merienda*.

"How long do they keep this thing up, without breaking down?" asked Thorpe, on the evening of the sixth day, and after another race where the women had screamed themselves hoarse, and one man had stabbed another. All were now fraternal and enthusiastic in a *cascarone* frolic.

"They are made of elastic, as far as pleasure is concerned," replied Estenega. "If they had to work six hours out of twenty-four, they would be haggard, and weak in the knees."

Thorpe entered the sala. The furniture, with the exception of the tables, had been removed; and men and women, with the abandon of children, were breaking eggshells, filled with cologne, tinsel, and flour, on the back of each other's heads. Black hair was flowing to the floor; white teeth were set behind arch tense lips; black eyes were snapping; nostrils were dilating. Even Doña Eustaquia and Chonita had joined in the romp. Prudencia, alone, ever mindful of her dignity, stood in a corner, the back of her head protected by the wall. She raised her fan to Thorpe, and he made his way to her under a shower of *cascarones*. The cologne ran down his neck, and made a paste of flour and tinsel on his head.

"Ay, señor!" exclaimed the châtelaine of Casa Grande, as he bowed before her. "No is unbecome at all. How you like the way we make the fun?"

Thorpe assured her that life was unmitigated amusement for the first time.

"No? You no laughing at us, señor?"

"It has been my good fortune to laugh with you for six days."

"Si: I theenk you like. I watching you." Prudencia gave her head a coquettish toss.

She was still a very pretty woman, despite her flesh.

"Oh, now you flatter me awfully. Why should you watch your most insignificant guest?"

"You no are the more — how you call him? — eens — *bueno! no importa.* You are the more honour guest I have. Si you like California, Señor Torp, why you no living here?"

"Oh — I — " He had heard that question before, in different circumstances. He was standing with his back to the wall. The brilliant picture before him became the mise-en-scène of an opera, the babble of voices its chorus. To his reversed vision, it crowded backward and cohered. And upon its shifting front, upon the wall of light and laughter and beauty, was projected the tragic figure of Nina Randolph.

Thorpe felt that his dark face was visibly paling. A small angry fist seemed to strike his heart, and all his being ached with sudden pity and longing.

A soft hand brushed his. He turned with a start and looked down into the coquettish eyes of his hostess. He noted mechanically that she had a very determined mouth, and that her colour was higher than usual.

"I beg pardon?" he stammered.

"Why you no stay here?" whispered Prudencia.

"Well, I may, you know; my plans are very unsettled."

"You ever been marry, señor?"

"No, señora."

"I have; and I love the husband, before; but so many years that ees now. You think ees possiblee keep on love when the other have been dead twenty years?"

"I think so."

"Ay! So I theenk once. But no was intend, I theenk, to live 'lone alway."

"Then why have you never married again, dear señora!" Thorpe found the conversation very tiresome.

"Ay! The men here—all are alike the one to the other. Never I marry another Californian."

"Ah!"

"No!"

His restless eyes suddenly encountered

hers. He felt the blood climb to his hair, his breath come short. His hands desperately sought his pockets.

"I am sure, if you went to San Francisco, you would be overwhelmed with offers — from Americans. This room is frightfully warm, don't you think so, señora? Shall I open the door? Ah, what a nuisance! here comes Don Adan Menendez to talk to you, and two other admirers are in his wake. I must release you for the moment. *Hasta luego*, dear señora!"

He made his way rapidly down the room, and out of the house.

"Great heaven!" he thought. "It is well the week is over. Good God, what a travesty!" and he laughed aloud.

He passed through the screaming crowd, which also had its *cascarones*, and walked rapidly and aimlessly up the valley until the white placid walls of the Mission were so close that he could count its arches. He sat down on a rock, and pressed his hands against his head.

He resented the quiet and beauty of the night, the repose of the Mission, the dark-blue spangled sky, the soft sobbing of the ocean. If Queen Mab and her train had come down to dance on the brink of hell, the antithesis could not have jarred more hatefully than the night upon his thoughts. He felt a desire to strike something, and hit the rock with his fist. He dug his heel into the ground, then thought of the flour and tinsel on his hair, and laughed aloud. After a time he put his face into his hands and wept. The sobs convulsed him, straining his muscles; the tears seemed wrung from some inner frozen fountain.

The storm passed. Calmer, he sat and thought. His love for Nina Randolph, during this interval of quiescence, had lost nothing of its iron. Idealised, she came back to him. Or, rather, he told himself he looked through the husk that the hideous circumstances of her life had bundled into shape, to the soul which spoke to his own. He worshipped her courage. He forgot himself and suffered with her. He hated himself for not having guessed the truth at once, and borne her burden. True, she had lied to him; but the lie was pardonable, and he attached no significance to it. If she had loved him less, she would have confessed the truth, indifferently. Others knew.

Her moods passed in review, with keen allurement. He wondered that he had ever wished her a woman of even and tangible temperament. The thought of her variety intoxicated him. The very equilibrium of the world might be disturbed, but he would have her.

The horror of her impending fate jibbered at him. He set his teeth, and compelled his mind to practical deduction. Her mother was only insane at intervals; there was no reason why the daughter should be affected in a dissimilar manner. Why, indeed, should not her attacks be far less frequent, if she were happy and her life were alternately peaceful and diversified? He would have the best advice in Europe, and guard her unremittingly.

His impulse was to return to her at once. He cogitated until dawn, then concluded to take her father's advice in part; he would remain awav a month, then come down upon her unexpectedly. But he went to his room and wrote her a letter, begging for a word in return.

XXI

EARLY in the forenoon he started northward with the Brothertons and Estenegas. Reinaldo kissed him on both cheeks, much to his embarrassment; but Prudencia accepted his farewells with chilling dignity, and did not invite him to return.

The Rancho de los Pinos was some ten miles from Monterey. Behind the house was a pine forest whose outposts were scattered along the edge of the Pacific; facing it were some eight thousand acres of rolling land, cut with willowed creeks, studded with groves of oaks, dazzling, at this season, with the gold of June. Thousands of cattle wandered about in languid content; the air lay soft and heavy on unquiet pulses.

The Brothertons and their guests "horsebacked" in the morning, but spent the greater part of the day in the hammocks swung across the long cool corridors. After supper, they rambled through the woods, sometimes as far as the ocean, where they sat on the rocks until midnight. The conversation rarely wandered from politics; for it was the summer of 1860, and the approaching national earthquake rumbled loudly. Nevertheless, life on the Rancho de los Pinos was less in touch with the world than any part of the strange new land which Thorpe had visited; and he hardly felt an impulse to speed the lagging moments. Doña Eustaquia, who had been one of the very pulses of the old régime, still beat with loud and undiminished vigour; but Chonita was very restful, and the country enfolded one with a large sleepy content. He received nothing from Nina Randolph, but her father wrote once or twice saying that she was well, but taking little interest in the summer gaieties.

On the first of July, he took the boat from Monterey to San José. There he was the guest of Don Tiburcio Castro for a few days, and attended a bull fight, a race at which the men bet the very clothes off their backs, a religious festival, and three balls; then took the stage which passed Redwoods on its way to San Francisco. It was a ride of thirty miles under a blistering sun, through dust twelve inches deep which the heavy hoofs of the horses and the wheels of the lumbering coach tossed ten feet in the air, half smothering the inside passengers, and coating those on top within and without. Thorpe had secured the seat by the driver, thinking to forget the physical discomforts in the scenery. But the tame prettiness of the valley was obliterated by the shifting wall of dust about the stage; and Thorpe closed his eyes, and resigned himself to misery. Even the driver would not talk, beyond observing that it was "the goldarndest hottest day he'd ever knowed, and that was saying a darned sight, *you* bet!" It was late in the afternoon when the stage pulled up at the "hotel" of a little village.

"That there's Redwoods," said the driver, pointing with his whip toward a mass of trees on rising ground. "Evenin'. I wish I wuz you."

The hotel seemed principally saloon; but the proprietor, who was chewing vigorously, told Thorpe he guessed he could accommodate him, and led him to a small room whose very walls were crackling with the heat. Thorpe distinctly saw the fleas jumping on the bare boards, and shuddered.

"Can I have a bath?" he asked.

"A what?"

"A bath."

"Oh!—we don't pronounce it that way in these parts. And bath-tubs is a luxury you'll have to go to 'Frisco for, I guess."

"Hav'n't you any sort of a tub you could bring me? I have a call to pay, and I must clean up."

"Perhaps the ole woman'd let you have one of her wash-tubs. I'll ask her."

"Do. And I should like supper as soon after as possible."

The old woman contributed the tub. It leaked, and it was redolent of coarse soap and the indigo that escapes from overalls. Thorpe got rid of his dust; but the smells, and the hot room, and the cloud of dust that sprang back from his clothes as he shook them out of the window, improved neither his aching head nor his temper. To make matters worse, the steak for his supper was fried, the potatoes were swimming in grease, the butter was rancid, and the piecrust hung down with its own weight. He ate what little of this typical repast he could in a close low room, crowded with men in their shirt-sleeves, who expectorated freely, mopped their faces and necks with their napkins, and smelt. The flies swarmed, a million strong, and invaded the very plates; a previous battalion lay, gasping or dead, on the tables, some overcome by the heat, others by the sharp assaults of angry napkins. When Thorpe left the room, he had half made up his mind not to call on Nina Randolph that evening; he felt in anything but a loverlike mood. Moreover, such an introduction to a reunion was grotesque; but after he had smoked his cigar in the open air, he felt better, concluded not to be a romantic ass, and started for the house.

He climbed the dusty road toward the two tall redwoods (the only ones in the valley) that gave her home its name, then turned into a long cool avenue. Beside it ran a creek, dry already, its sides thick with fragrant shrubs. So closely planted was the avenue that he did not catch a glimpse of the house until he came suddenly upon it; then he paused a moment, regarding it with pleasure. It looked like a fairy castle, so light and delicate and mediæval of structure was it. The yellow plaster of its walls, the vivid bloom of the terrace on which it stood, were plainly visible in the moonlight. The dark mountains, covered with their redwood forests, seemed almost directly behind, although they were twenty miles away. Thorpe was glad he had come. The hideous afternoon and evening slipped out of his thought.

The front doors were open. Cochrane was walking up and down the hall, his hands clasped behind him, his head bent. He looked like a man who was listlessly awaiting a summons.

Light streamed from open windows to the verandah on the right of the house. Thorpe, conceiving that Nina was there, determined to look upon her for a moment unobserved. He skirted the house, and heard Nina's voice.

To command a view of the interior, he must reach the verandah. He mounted the steps softly, but other sounds rose high above his footfalls as he walked toward the window. A peal of coarse laughter burst forth. The light swept obliquely across the verandah; he stood in the shadows just beyond it, and looked into the room.

Nina sat in a corner, her elbows on her knees, her eyes fixed on the floor. Her black dress was destitute of any feminine device. Mrs. Randolph and Mrs. Reinhardt sat on opposite sides of a table. Between them was a steaming bowl of punch. There were two unopened brandy-bottles on the table. The faces of both women were flushed, and their hair was disordered.

"Tha 't a fool, Nina," remarked Mrs. Randolph, in a remarkably steady tone. "Coom and 'ave a glass. My word! it 's good."

Nina made no reply.

"Such nonsense," wheedlingly. "It's the best a iver made, and the Lord knows a 've made mony. Coom and try just one glass."

"I am sitting here to test my strength. I shall not touch it."

Mrs. Randolph laughed, coarsely and loudly. "Tha 't a fool. Tha doon't knoo what tha't talking aboot. It strikes me a 've 'eard thot before. Coom. Tha mought as well give in, fust as last."

Nina made no reply.

Mrs. Randolph's evil eyes sparkled. She filled an empty glass with the punch, and walked steadily over to where her daughter sat. Nina sprang from her chair, overturning it, thrusting out her hands in a gesture eloquent with terror, and attempted to reach the door. Mrs. Randolph was too quick for her; with a dexterous swoop, she possessed herself of the girl's small hands and pressed the goblet to her nostrils. Nina gave a quick gasp, and, throwing back her head, staggered slightly, the glass still against her face. Outside Thorpe reeled for a moment as if he too were drunk. The blood pounded in his ears; his fingers drew inward, rigid, in their desire to get about the throat of some one, he did not much care whom.

Nina wrenched one hand free, snatched

the goblet and held it with crooked elbow, staring at her mother. Mrs. Randolph laughed. Mrs. Reinhardt held her breath in drunken awe at the tragedy in the girl's face. Nina brought the goblet half way to her lips, her eyes moving to its warm brown surface with devouring greed. Then she flung it at her mother's breast, and sank once more to her chair, covering her face with her hands.

Mrs. Randolph, cursing, returned to the table and consoled herself with a brimming glass. Outside, the man's imagination played him an ugly trick. A picture flashed upon it, vivid as one snatched from the dark by the blaze of lightning. A struggling distorted foaming thing was on the floor, held down by the strong arms of two men, and the face of the thing was not the face of Mrs. Randolph. She stood apart, looking down upon her perfected work with a low continuous ripple of contented laughter. The vision passed. Thorpe leaped from the verandah and wandered aimlessly about the grounds. He cursed audibly and repeatedly, not caring whether he might be overheard or not. He felt as if every nerve in his body were a separate devil. He hated the thought of the next day's sunlight, and wondered if it would shine on a murderer or a suicide; he felt capable of crime of the blackest variety.

Fascinated, he returned to the verandah. Mrs. Randolph had fallen forward on the table. The man Cochrane entered and took her by the shoulders. She flung out her arm and struck him.

"Give oop! Give oop!" she muttered. But he jerked her backward, and half dragged, half carried her from the room. Mrs. Reinhardt staggered after, slamming the door behind her. Then Nina rose and came forward, and leaned her finger-tips heavily on the table.

"Come in," she said; and Thorpe entered.

They faced each other in silence. For a moment Thorpe was conscious only of the change in her. Her cheeks were sunken and without colour; her eyes patched about with black. The features were so controlled that they were almost expressionless.

"Sit down," she said. "I will tell you the story."

He took the chair Mrs. Reinhardt had occupied, Nina her mother's. She pressed her knuckles against her cheeks, and began speaking rapidly, but without excitement.

"My father's home in Yorkshire was near the town of Keighley, which is a few miles from Haworth, the village where the Brontës lived. He and Branwell Brontë were great friends, and used to meet at the Lord Rodney Inn in Keighley, as Haworth is an almost inaccessible place. They were both very brilliant young men; and many other young men used to drop in on Saturday evenings to hear them talk politics. Of course the night ended in a bout, which usually lasted over Sunday. My mother was bar-maid at that inn. She made up her mind to marry my father. It is said that at that time she was handsome. She had an insatiable thirst for liquor, but was clever enough to keep my father from suspecting it. Once my father — who cared little for drink, beyond the conviviality of it — and Brontë went on a prolonged spree, the result of a bet. When he came to himself, he found that he had married her before the registrar. He belonged to one of the oldest families in the county. He had married a woman who could neither read nor write, and who talked at all times as she does now when she is drunk. Nevertheless, he determined to stand by her, because he thought he deserved his fate, and because he thought she loved him. But he left the country. To introduce her to his people and friends was more than he was equal to. To bury himself with her on his estate, denying himself all society but hers, was equally unthinkable, to say nothing of the fact that he was ashamed to introduce her to the servants. He wished to go away and be forgotten, begin life over in a new land where social conditions were as the builders made them. He came to California. She was furious. She had married him for the position she had fancied such a marriage would give her: she wanted to be a lady. Her mind was somewhat diverted by travel, and she kept her peace until she reached San Francisco —

Yerba Buena, it was called then. It was a tiny place: a few adobe houses about the plaza, and a warehouse or two at the docks. Then there was a frightful scene between the two. My father learned why she had married him, and that she had instigated the wager which led to the spree which enabled her to accomplish her purpose. She ordered him to take her back to England at once, threatening to punish him if he did not. He refused, and she went on a prolonged drinking bout. This was shortly before my birth. They were the guests of Mr. Leese, a German who had married a native Californian and settled in the country. These people were very kind; but it was horribly mortifying for my father. He built her a house as quickly as possible, in order to hide her in it. I forgot to say that he had brought over Cochrane, who took charge of his household affairs. At the end of a year there was another scene, in which my father made her understand that he would never return to England; and that, were it not for me, he would turn her out of the house and let her go to the devil as fast as she liked. It was the mistake of his life that he did not, both for himself and for me. He should have taken or sent me back to England, and left her with a subsistence in the new country. But he is a very proud man. He feared that she would follow him home, and publish the story. There is no getting away from a woman like that.

"She was forced to accept the position; but she hated him mortally, and no less than he hated her. She had threatened again to make him rue his refusal to return to England, but refused to explain her meaning. This is what she did. He idolised me. She put whisky in my baby food until I would not drink or eat anything that was not flavoured with it. She was very cunning: she habituated my system to it gradually, so that it never upset me. She also gave it to me for every ailment. My father suspected nothing. There were depths of depravity that neither his imagination nor his observation plumbed. When I was about thirteen, he left us in charge of Cochrane—who had more influence over my mother than any one—and went off to the Crimean war, rejoining his old regiment. The necessity to get away from her for a time overrode his paternal instinct—everything. Moreover, he wanted to fight somebody. He distinguished himself. Just after his return, he discovered what my mother had made of me. His rage was awful; he beat her like a navvy. For once she was cowed. I went off my head altogether. When I came to, he was crouching in a corner as if some one had flung him there, sobbing and gasping. It was awful—awful! Then he sent me to the Hathaways to study with the girls. They knew, and promised to keep me away from her, and to see that I had nothing to drink. My mother sent me a bottle of whisky every week in my clean clothes. I did not tell him, for I wanted it. He found that out, too, and then debated whether he had not better send me away from the country. But he knew that the cry was in my blood, and that if I went to his people in England the chances were I would disgrace him. Then he made his second mistake: he did not throw her out. He ordered her to go, and she laughed in his face and asked him how he would like to read every morning in the *Golden Era* that James Randolph's wife had spent the night in the calaboose. Now, only two or three people besides the Hathaways and Shropshires even suspected it, so carefully had Cochrane watched her.

"He sent me to boarding-school. She kept me in money, and I got what I wanted, although my father's pride was in me, and I never took enough to betray my secret. It was not until I had finished school that I really gave way to the appetite. My father, closely as he watched me, did not suspect for a long time. He was very busy, — he threw himself heart and soul into the development of the city, — and when the appetite mastered me, I either feigned illness or went to the country. At last he found it out. There have been many bitter hours in my life, but that was incomparably the bitterest. I had always loved him devotedly. When he went down on his knees and begged me to stop, of course I swore that I would. I kept my promise for six months, she doing all she could to entice me the while. Then I yielded. After that, after another interview with my father, I restrained the intolerable craving for another six months. Then it went on irregularly. I don't know that I began to think much, to look into the future, until about a year ago — it was when I first saw her as you saw her that night. Then I aged suddenly. My moral sense awakened, my sense of personal responsibility. I loathed myself. I looked upon what I had become with horror. I struggled fiercely, — but with indifferent success, — although, I must add, there were weeks at a time when I never thought of it; for I have the *joie de vivre*, and there are many distractions in society. Then you came. For a time I was happy and excited, and the thing was in abeyance. I touched nothing: that was my only chance. I fought it under, — after that first night, — and the desire did not come again until I drank the mescal at Don Tiburcio's *merienda*. But I had known that it would come back sooner or later, and was determined not to marry you, nor to let myself fall seriously in love with you. But after that first night out on the strawberry patches I knew that I loved you, and, as I am not a light-minded person, irrevocably. But I made up my mind to enjoy that week, and look no farther. You know the rest. What I have suffered since perhaps you can divine, if you love me. If you don't, it does n't matter." Her monotonous calm left her suddenly. She brought her fist down on the table. "This room is full of the smell of it!" she cried. "And I want it! I want it!"

She pushed back her chair. "Come," she said, "let us go outside."

She ran out to the verandah. He followed, and she grasped his arm. "Let us go for a ride," she said. "I shall go off my head, if I keep still another moment. I want motion. Are you tired?"

"No, I am not tired."

She led the way to the stables. The men in charge had gone to bed. She and Thorpe saddled two strong mustangs, rode rapidly down the avenue and out into the high road. For some time they followed the stage-route, then struck into a side road leading to the mountains. Nina did not speak, nor did Thorpe. He was thankful for the respite. Once he touched his cheek mechanically, wondering if it had fallen into wrinkles.

They rode at a break-neck pace. The night had become very dark: a great ocean of fog had swept in from the Pacific, blotting out mountains and stars. The mustangs moderated their pace as they began to ascend the foot-hills. The long rush through the valley had quickened Thorpe's blood without calming his brain. He did not speak. There seemed to be a thousand words struggling in his brain, but they would not combine properly. He could have cursed them free, but although he was too bitter and excited to have tenderness or pity for the woman beside him, he considered her in a half blind way: she was the one woman on earth who had ever sent him utterly beside himself. They ascended, two black spots of shifting outline in the fog, for an hour or more. Neither below nor above could an object be seen, not a sound came to them. It was unreal, and ghostly, and portentous. Then, almost abruptly, they emerged, the mustangs trotting on to the flat summit of a hill. Nina sprang to the ground.

"Tie the horses," she said; and Thorpe led them to a tree some yards away.

Nina stood with her back to him, her hands hanging listlessly at her sides, looking downward. Thorpe, after he had tethered the horses, paused also.

The world below was gone. In its place was a vast ocean of frothy milk-white fog. On each side, melting into the horizon in front, until it washed the slopes of the Contra Costa range, lay this illimitable ocean pillowed lightly on sleeping millions. Now calm and peaceful, now distorted in frozen wrath, it was so shadowy, so unreal, that a puff of wind might have blown it to the stars. Out of it rose the hill-tops, bare weather-beaten islands. Against them the sea had hurled itself, then clung, powerless to retreat. Upon some it had cast its spray half way to the crest, over others it rushed in mighty motionless torrents; here and there it but half concealed the jagged points of ugly rocks. Beating against solitary reefs were huge, still, angry breakers, sounding no roar. A terrible death-arrested storm was there in mid-ocean, — a storm which appalled by its very silent wrath. On one of the highest and barest of the crags an old building looked, in that sunless light, like a castle in ruin. Above, the cold blue sky was thickly set with shivering stars. The grinning moon hung low.

There was not a sound; not a living creature was awake but themselves. They might have been in the shadowy hereafter, with all space about them; in the twilight of eternity. Where they rested, the air was clear as a polar noon; not a stray wreath of that idle froth floated about them.

"I came here," said Nina, turning to Thorpe, "because I knew it would be like this. It will be easier to hear what you think of me, than it would have been down there."

He brought his hands down on her shoulders, gripping them as if possessed of the instinct to hurt.

"Once or twice I could have killed you as you spoke," he said. "I shall marry you and cure you, or go to hell with you. As I feel now, it does not matter much which."

And then he caught her in his arms and kissed her, with the desire which was consuming him.

"But even you cannot conquer me," she said to him an hour later. "I shall not marry you until I have conquered myself. I believe now that I can. I got your letter. I very nearly knew that you would say what you have done, after I told you the truth. I won't marry you, knowing that, in spite of your love, which I do not doubt, at the bottom of your intelligence, you despise me. I have always felt that if I could make a year's successful fight, I should never fall again. There may be no reason for this belief; but we are more or less controlled by imagination. There is no doubt in my mind on this point. If I win alone, you will respect me again, and love me better."

"I do not despise you. I hardly know what I felt for you five weeks ago. But I have only sympathy for you now — and love! You must let me do the fighting. It will knit us the more closely —"

"It would wear me out, kill me, knowing that you were watching my struggles, no matter how lovingly. Besides, I know myself; my moods are unbearable at such times. I cannot control my temper. Before the year was over, we should have bickered our love into ruins. We could not begin over again. If you will do as I wish, I believe we can be happy. It is not long to wait — we are both young. Cannot you see that I am right?"

"I don't want to leave you, not for a day again!"

"And I don't want you to go! But I know that it is our only chance. If you marry me now, you will hate me before the year is over; and, what is worse, I shall hate you. The steamer sails to-morrow. Will you go?"

He hesitated, and argued, a long while; but finally he said: "I will go."

"Don't go all the way back to England. I should like to think you were in America; that would help me."

"I will stay in New Orleans, and write by every steamer."

"Oh, do, do! And if I do not write as regularly, you will understand. There will be times when I simply cannot write. But promise that, no matter what you hear, you will not lose faith in me."

"I promise." Involuntarily his mouth curled into a grin. The ghosts of a respectable company of extorted promises capered across his brain, as small irreverent ghosts have a habit of doing in great moments. But his mouth was close upon hers, and she did not see it.

An hour later she pointed outward. Far away, above the Eastern mountains, was a line of flame. The sun rose slowly. It smiled down upon the phantom ocean and flung bubbles of a thousand hues to the very feet of the mortals on the heights.

Then slowly, softly, the ocean moved. It quivered as if a mighty hand struck it from its foundations, swayed, rose, fled back to the sea that had given it birth.

A moment more and the world was visible again, awake, and awaiting them.

BOOK II

BOOK II

I

Mr. Randolph owned a large ranch in Lake County which was managed by an agent. A mile distant from the farm-house in which the agent lived with the "hands" was a cottage, built several years since at Nina's request. As Lake County was then difficult of access, Mr. Randolph seldom visited his ranch, his wife never; but once a year Nina took a party of girl friends to the cottage, usually in mid-summer. This year she went alone. Immediately after Thorpe's departure she told her father of the conditional engagement into which she had entered.

"And I wish to spend this year alone," she added. "Not only because I want to get away from my mother, but because I believe that nothing will help me more than entire change of associations. And solitude has no terrors for me. I simply cannot go on in the old routine. I am bored to death with the meaninglessness of it. That has come suddenly: probably because I have come to want so much more."

"But would n't you rather travel, Nina?" Mr. Randolph was deeply anxious; he hardly knew whether to approve her plan or not. A year's solitude would drive him to madness.

"No, I want to live with myself. If I rushed from one distraction to another I should not feel sure of myself at the end. I have thought and thought; and, besides, I want to see and live Europe with Dudley Thorpe alone. I feel positive that my plan is the right one. Only keep my mother away."

"I will tell her plainly that if she follows you, I 'll shut her up in the Home of the Inebriates; and this time I 'll keep my word. What excuse shall you give people?"

"You can tell them of my engagement, and say that as we have agreed it shall last a year, I have my own reasons for spending the interval by myself. Their comments mean nothing to me."

"Shall you see no one?"

"Molly will come occasionally, and you,— no one else. I shall fish and hunt and sail and ride and read and study music. Perhaps you will send me a little piano?"

"Of course I will."

"I shall live out of doors mostly. I love that sort of life better than any; I like trees better than most people."

"Very well. If you change your mind, you have only to return. I will send to New York for all the new books and music. Cochrane will go ahead and put things in order. I will also send Atkins to look after the horses; and he and his wife will sleep in the house and look after you generally. I hope to God the experiment will prove a success. I think you are wise not to marry until the fight is over."

II

THE cottage was on the side of a hill overlooking one of the larger lakes. Beyond were other lakes, behind and in front the pine-covered mountains. The place was very wild; it was doubtful if civilisation would ever make it much less so. The cottage was dainty and comfortable. Nina sailed a little cat-boat during the cooler hours of the day; and she was a good shot. She wrote a few lines or pages every night to Thorpe; but it was several days before she opened a book. She roamed through the dark forests while it was hot, and in the evenings. She had for California that curious compound of hatred and adoration which it inspires in all highly strung people who know it well. It filled her with vague angry longings, inspired her at times with a fierce desire to flee from it, and finally; but it satisfied her soul. At times, a vast brooding peace seemed lying low over all the land. At others, she fancied she could hear mocking laughter.

More than once she hung out of the window half the night, expecting that California would lift up her voice and speak, so tremendous is the personality of that strange land. She longed passionately for Thorpe.

The weeks passed, and, to her astonishment, the poison in her blood made no sign. Three months, and there had not been so much as a skirmish with the enemy. She felt singularly well; so happy at times that she wondered at herself, for the year seemed very long. Thorpe wrote by every steamer, such letters as she had hoped and expected to get. Some of his vital personality seemed to emanate from them; and she chose to believe that it stood guard and warned off the enemy.

She was swinging in her hammock on the verandah one hot afternoon, when a wagon lumbered to the foot of the hill, and her father and Molly Shropshire emerged from the cloud of dust that surrounded it. She tumbled out of the hammock, and ran down to meet them, her loose hair flying.

"She looks about ten," thought Mr. Randolph, as she rushed into his arms; "and beautiful for the first time in her life."

"We thought that you had had as much solitude as was good for you at one time," said Miss Shropshire, in her hard metallic voice, which, however, rang very true. "I am going to stay a month, whether I am wanted or not."

"We have an addition to our family," said Mr. Randolph, as he sat fanning himself on the piazza. "Your cousin has arrived."

"My what? What cousin?"

"Your mother, it seems, has a brother. If I ever knew of his existence, I had forgotten it. But it seems that I have had the honour of educating his son and of transforming him into a sort of pseudo-gentleman."

"He is not half bad, indeed," said Miss Shropshire.

"He is the sort of man who inspires me with a desire to lift my boot every time he opens his mouth. But I must confess that his appearance is fairly creditable. The obsolete term 'genteel' describes him better than any other. He has got Yorkshire off his back, has studied hard, — he is a doctor with highly creditable certificates and diplomas, — and dresses very well. His manners are suave, entirely too suave: I felt disposed to warn the bank; and his hands are so soft that they give me a 'turn' as the old women say. He has reddish hair, a pale grey shifty eye, a snub nose, and a hollow laugh. There you have your cousin — Dr. Richard Clough, aged twenty-eight or thereabouts. In my days, he probably wore clogs. At present his natty little feet are irreproachably shod, and he makes no more noise than a cat. I feel an irrepressible desire for a caricature of him."

Nina laughed heartily. "Poor papa! And you thought you had had the last of the Cloughs. I hope he is not quartered on you."

"He is, but is looking about for an opening. To do him justice, I don't think he is a sponge. He seems to have saved something. He wanted to come up here and pay his *devoirs* to you, but I evaded the honour. I have a personal suspicion which may, of course, be wide of the mark, that the object of his visit to California is more matrimonial than professional; if that is the case, he might cause you a great deal of annoyance: there is a very ugly look about his mouth."

Mr. Randolph remained several days; they were very happy days for him. It was impossible to see Nina as she was at that period, to catch the overflow of her spirits, without sharing her belief in the sure happiness of the future.

Miss Shropshire fell in easily with all of Nina's pursuits. There was much of Nina Randolph that she could never understand; but she was as faithful as a dog in her few friendships and, with her vigorous sensible mind, she was a companion who never bored. She was several years older than Nina. Their fathers had been acquaintances in the island which had the honour of incubating the United States.

"I approve of your engagement," said Miss Shropshire, in her downright way. "I know if I don't you will hate me, so I have brought myself to the proper frame of mind. He is selfish; but he certainly grows on one, and no one could help respecting a man with that jaw."

But Nina would not discuss Thorpe even with Molly Shropshire. When she felt obliged to unburden her mind, she went up and talked to the pines.

The girls returned home one morning from a stiff sail on the lake to be greeted by the sight of a boot projecting beyond the edge of one of the hammocks, and the perfume of excellent tobacco.

"What on earth!" exclaimed Miss Shropshire. "Have we a visitor? a man?"

Nina frowned. "I suspect that it is my cousin. Papa wrote the other day that Richard had heard of a practice for sale in Napa, and had come up to look into it. I suppose it was to be expected that he would come here, whether he was invited or not."

As the girls ascended the hill, the occupant of the hammock rose and flung away his cigar. He was a dapper little man, and walked down the steep path with a jaunty ease which so strikingly escaped vulgarity as to suggest the danger.

"Dear Cousin Nina!" he exclaimed "Miss Shropshire, you will tell her that I am Richard? Will you pardon me for taking two great liberties, — first, coming here, and then, taking possession of your hammock and smoking? The first I *could n't* help. The last — well, I have been waiting two hours."

"I am glad you have made yourself at home," said Nina, perfunctorily; she had conceived a violent dislike for him. "Your trip must have been very tiresome."

"It was, indeed. This California is all very well to look at, but for travelling comforts — my word! However, I am not regretting. I cannot tell you how much I have wanted — "

"You must be very hungry. There is the first dinner-bell. Are you dusty? Would you like to clean up? Go to papa's room — that one.

"Detestable man!" she said, as he disappeared. "I don't believe particularly in presentiments, but I felt as if my evil genius were bearing down upon me. And such a smirk! He looks like a little shop-keeper."

"I think he cultivates that grin to conceal the natural expression of his mouth — which is by no means unlike a wolf's. But he is a harmless little man enough, I have no doubt. I've been hasty and mistaken too often; only it's a bore, having to entertain him."

But Dr. Clough assumed the burdens of entertaining. He talked so agreeably during dinner, told Nina so much of London that she wished to know, betrayed such an exemplary knowledge of current literature, that her aversion was routed for the hour, and she impulsively invited him to remain a day or two. He accepted promptly, played a nimble game of croquet after supper, then took them for a sail on the lake. He had a thin well-trained tenor voice which blended fairly well with Miss Shropshire's metallic soprano; and the two excited the envy of the frogs and the night-birds. He was evidently a man quick to take a hint, for he treated Nina exactly as he treated Molly: he was merely a traveller in a strange land, delighted to find himself in the company of two charming women.

"Upon my word," said Molly, that night, "I rather like the little man. He's not half bad."

"I don't know," said Nina. "I'm sorry I asked him to stay. I'll be glad to see him go."

The next day he organised a picnic, and made them sit at their ease while he cooked and did all the work. They spent the day in a grove of laurels, and sailed home in the dusk. It was on the following day that Nina twice caught him looking at her in a peculiarly searching manner. Each time she experienced a slight chill and faintness, for which she was at a loss to account. She reddened with anger and terror, and he shifted his eyes quickly. When he left, the next morning, she drew a long sigh of relief, then, without warning, began to sob hysterically.

"There is something about that man!" she announced to the alarmed Miss Shropshire. "What is it? Do you suppose he is a mesmerist? He gave me the most dreadful feeling at times. Oh, I wish Dudley were here!"

"Why don't you send for him?"

"I don't know! I don't know! I wish the year were over!"

"It is your own will that makes it a year. I don't see any sense in it, myself. I believe this climate, and being away from everything, has set you up. Why not send for him, and live here for some months longer? He is your natural protector, anyhow. What's a man good for?"

"Oh, I feel as if I must! Wait till to-morrow. That man has made me nervous; I may feel quite placid to-morrow, and I ought to wait. It is only right to wait."

And the next day she was herself again, and dismissed the evil spell of Dr. Clough with a contemptuous shrug. Nor would she send for Thorpe.

"I may cut it down to eight months," she said. "But I must wait that long."

III

A WEEK later Miss Shropshire returned to San Francisco. Nina was not sorry to be alone again. She drifted back into her communion with the inanimate things about her, into the exaltation of spirit, impossible in human companionship, and lived for Thorpe's letters.

One day she received a letter from Dr. Clough.

"DEAR COUSIN NINA," it ran. "I am to have the practice in Napa, but not for two or three months, unfortunately, for I look forward to meeting you again. Those few days with you and Miss Molly were delightful to the lonely wanderer, who has never known a home." ("Not since he wore clogs," thought Nina.) "Perhaps some day I shall make substantial acknowledgment of my gratitude. This is a world of vicissitudes, as we all know. Remember this — will you, Nina?— when you need me *I am there.* There are crises in life when a true friend, a relative whose interests merge with one's own, is not to be despised. Don't destroy this letter. Put it by. It is sincere.

"Your faithful and obd't servant,

"RICHARD CLOUGH."

Nina tossed the letter impatiently on the table, then caught it up again and re-read the last pages.

"That sounds as if it were written *avec intention*," she thought. "Can papa be embarrassed? But what good could this scrubby little man do me, if he were? Most likely it is the first gun of the siege. Thank Heaven the guns must be fired through the post for a while."

December was come, but it was still very warm. The lake was hard and still and blue. The glare was merciless.

Nina, followed by a servant bearing cushions, climbed wearily up the hill to the forest. Once or twice she paused and caught at a tree for support.

"If I ever get into the forest, I believe I 'll stay there until this weather is over," she thought. "It has completely demoralised me."

The servant arranged the cushions in a hammock between two pines whose arms locked high above, — a green fragrant roof the sun could not penetrate. Nina made herself comfortable, and re-read Thorpe's last letter, received the day before. It was a very impatient letter. He wanted her, and life in the South was a bore after the novelty had worn off.

She lay thinking of him, and listening to the drowsy murmur of forest life about her. Squirrels were chattering softly, somewhere in the arbours above those slender grey pillars. A confused hum rose from the ground; from far came the roar of a torrent. She could see the blue lake with its ring of white sand, the bluer sky above, and turned her back: the sight brought heat into those cool depths. Above her rose the dim green aisles, the countless columns of the forest. She was very tired and languid. She placed Thorpe's letter under her cheek and slept; and in her sleep she dreamed.

She was still in the forest: every lineament of it was familiar. For a time there were none of the changes of dreams. Then from the base of every pine something lifted slowly and coiled about the tree, — something long and green and horridly beautiful. It lifted itself to the very branches, then detached itself a little and waved a foot of its upper length to and fro, its glittering eyes regarding her with sleepy malice. The squirrels had hidden in their caves; not a sound came from the earth; the waters had hushed their voice. Nothing moved in that awful silence but the languid heads of the snakes.

Then came a sudden brisk step; her cousin entered. He did not notice the sleeper, but went to each constrictor in turn and stroked it lovingly. Once he caught a coil close to his breast and laughed. The small malignant eyes above moved to his, their expression changing to friendliness, albeit shot with contempt. To Nina's agonised sense the scene lasted for hours, during which Clough fondled the reptiles with increasing ardour.

But at last the scene changed, and abruptly. She was on the mountain above the fog-ocean, close to the stars. Thorpe's arms were strong about her. It had seemed to her in the past five months that she had never really ceased to feel the strength of his embrace, to hear the loud beating of his heart on her own. This time he withdrew one arm and, thrusting his fingers among her heartstrings, pulled them gently. Something vibrated throughout her. She had been happy before, but that soft vibration filled her with a new and inexplicable gladness. She asked him what it meant. He murmured something she could not understand, and smote the chords again. Her being seemed filled with music.

She awoke. The woods were dark. She tried to recall the ugly prelude to her dream, but it had passed. She put her hands against her shoulders, fancying she must encounter the arms that had held her, for their pressure lingered. Then she drew her brows together, and craned her neck with an expression of wonder. But several moments passed before she understood. She was very ignorant of many things, and her experience up to the present had been exceptional.

But she was a woman, and in time she understood.

Her first mental response was a wild unreasoning terror, that of the woman who is in sore straits, far from the man who should protect her and evoke the hasty sanction of the law. But the mood passed. She was sure of Thorpe, and she had all the arrogance of wealth. He would hasten at her summons, and they would live in this solitude for a year or more; no one beyond the necessary confidants need ever know.

The maternal instinct had awakened in her dream. She folded herself suddenly in her own arms. Her imagination flew to the future. Every imaginative woman who loves the man that becomes her husband must have one enduring regret: that in a third or more of his life she had no part; he grew to manhood knowing nothing of her little share in the scheme of things, met her when two at least of his personalities were coffined in the yesterday that is the most vivid of all the memories. And if his child be a boy, she may fancy it the incarnation of her husband's lost boyhood and youth, and thus complete the circle of her manifold desire.

And then Nina knew what had scotched the monster of heredity; she could see the tiny hands at its throat. She lay and marvelled until the servants, alarmed, came to look for her. The world took on a new and wonderful aspect; she was the most wonderful thing in it.

IV

After supper she went into the sitting-room and wrote to Thorpe. As she finished and left the desk, her eye fell on Richard Clough's letter, which lay, open, on the table. The same chill horror caught her as when she had encountered his searching eyes on the last day of his visit, and she understood its meaning. He knew; there was the key to his verbiage.

She dropped upon a chair, feeling faint and ill. Like many women, she had firm trust in her intuitions. If they had seemed baseless before, they rested on a firm enough foundation now. She was in this man's power; and the man was an adventurer and a Clough. Would he tell her father? Or worse — her mother! She pictured her father's grief; his rage against Thorpe. It would be more than she could endure. When Thorpe came, it would not matter so much. And if her father were not told, it was doubtful if he would ever suspect: he was very busy, and hated the trip from San Francisco to Lake County. After Thorpe's arrival, it was hardly likely that he would visit her.

A few moments' reflection convinced her that Clough would keep her secret. His was the mind of subtle methods. He would make use of his power over her in ways beyond her imagining.

Terror possessed her, and she called loudly upon Thorpe. With the sound of his name, her confidence returned. He would be with her in something under three months. Meanwhile, she could defy Clough. Later, he would meet more than his match.

The next day she wrote to Molly Shropshire, telling her the truth and giving her many commissions. Miss Shropshire's reply was characteristic:

"I have bought everything, and start for the cottage on Tuesday. It is fortunate that I have two married sisters; I can be of much assistance to you. I have helped on several wardrobes of this sort, and acquired much lore of which you appear to be painfully ignorant. I am coming with my large trunk; for I shall not leave you again."

The momentous subject was not broached for some hours after her arrival. Then — they were seated before the fire in the sitting-room, and the first rain of winter was pelting the roof — Miss Shropshire opened her mouth and spoke with vicious emphasis.

"I hate men. There is not one I'd lift my finger to do a service for. My sisters are supposed to have good husbands. One — Fred Lester — is a grown-up baby, full of whims and petty vanities and blatant selfishness, who has to be 'managed.' Tom Manning is as surly as a bear with a sore head when his dinner disappoints him; and when things go wrong in the office there is no living in the house with him. My brother's life is notorious, and his wife, what with patience and tears, looks like a pan of skim-milk. Catch me ever marrying! Not if Adonis came down and staked a claim about a mountain of gold quartz. As for Dudley Thorpe!" her voice rose to the pitch of fury. "What is a man's love good for, if it can't think of the woman first? Are n't they our natural protectors? Are n't they supposed to think for us, — take all the responsibilities of life off our shoulders? This sort of thing is in keeping with the character, is n't it? Why don't you hate him? You ought to. *I'd* murder him —"

Nina plunged across the rug, and pressed both hands against Miss Shropshire's mouth, her eyes blazing with passion.

"Don't you dare speak of him like that again! If you do, it will be the last time you will ever speak to me. I understand him — as well as if he were literally a part of myself. I 'll never explain to you nor to any one, but *I know*. And there is nothing in me that does not respond to him. Now, do you understand? Will you say another word?"

"Oh, very well. Don't stifle me!" Miss Shropshire released herself. "Have it that way, if it suits you best. I did n't come here to quarrel with you."

Nina resumed her seat. After a few moments she said: "There is another thing: Richard Clough knows." And she told Miss Shropshire of his letter.

"Um, well, I don't know but that that will be as good an arrangement as any. Some one must attend you, and a relative —"

"What! Do you think I'd have that reptile near me?"

"Now, Nina, look at the matter like a sensible woman. We shall have to get a doctor from Napa. If it storms, he may be days getting here. If he has a wife, she'll want to know where he has been, and will worm it out of him. If he has n't, he'll let it out some night when he has his feet on the table in his favourite saloon, and is outside his eighth glass of punch. It will be to Richard's interest to keep the matter quiet — you can make it his interest: I don't fancy he's above pocketing a couple of thousands. And he'll not dare annoy you after Dudley Thorpe is here. I'll do Dudley Thorpe this much justice: he could whip most men, and he would n't stop to think about it, either. Don't let us discuss the matter any further now. Just turn it over in your mind. I am sure you will come to the conclusion that I am right. If you ignore Richard, there's no knowing what he may do."

V

The next day Miss Shropshire cut out many small garments, Nina watching her with ecstatic eyes. Both were expert needlewomen, — most Californian girls were in those days of the infrequent and inferior dressmaker, — and in the weeks that came they fashioned many dainty and elegant garments. Nina no longer went to the forest, rarely on the lake. Miss Shropshire could hardly persuade her to go out once a day for a walk, so enthralled was she by that bewildering mass of fine linen and lace. She was prouder of her tucks than she had ever been of a semicircle of admirers, four deep; and when she had finished her first yoke she wept with delight.

Miss Shropshire often watched her curiously, half-comprehending. She abominated babies. Her home was with one of her married sisters, and a new baby meant the splitting of ear-drums, the foolish prattle and attenuated vocabulary of the female parent, and the systematic irritations of the inefficient nurse-maid. Why a woman should look as if heaven had opened its gates because she was going to have a baby, passed her comprehension, particularly in the embarrassing circumstances.

Nina was alone when Thorpe's next letter arrived.

"I am starting for Cuba," it began. "My brother Harold has joined me; and as his chest is in a bad way, he thinks of settling in a hot country. I have suggested California; but he is infatuated with the idea of Cuba. You will forgive me for leaving the United States for a short period, will you not, dearest? I can do you no particular good by remaining here, and I am bored to extinction. If you would but give me the word, I should start for California on the next steamer; but as you hold me to the original compact, perhaps you will give me a little latitude. The talk here is war, war, war, — never a variation by any possible chance. My sympathies are with the South, and if they fight I hope they 'll win; but as I have no personal interest in the matter I feel like a man condemned to a long course of one highly seasoned dish, with no prospect of variety. Address as usual; your letters will be forwarded, unless I return in a few weeks, as I think I shall." Then followed several closely written pages which advised her of the unalterable state of his affections.

Nina put the letter down, and stared before her with a wide introspective gaze. When Miss Shropshire entered, she handed her the first two pages. The older girl shut her lips.

"I don't like it," she said. "It means delay, and every week is precious. It looks—" She paused.

"Unlucky; I have been wondering. I have a queer helpless feeling, as if I were tangled in a net, and even Dudley, with all his love and will, could not get me out. I suppose there is something in fate. I feel very insignificant."

"Come, come, you are not to get morbid. Nobody's life is a straight line. You must expect hard knots, and rough byways, and malaria, and all the rest of it. Don't borrow trouble. You are sure of him, anyhow."

"Sometimes I hate California. One might as well be on Mars. It's thousands of miles from New Orleans, and New Orleans is hundreds of miles from Cuba. And now that everything is getting so upset, who knows if he'll ever get my letters? I wish I'd started straight for New Orleans the moment I knew. I am utterly at the mercy of circumstances."

"Well, thank Heaven you're rich," said Miss Shropshire, bluntly. "Just fancy if you were some poor little wretch deserted by the man, and with no prospect but the county hospital; then you might be blue."

"Oh, I suppose it might be worse!" replied Nina.

The next day her buoyant spirits were risen again, and she resolved to accept the immediate arrangement of her destiny with philosophy; peace and happiness would be hers eventually. She could not violate the most jealous of social laws and expect all the good fairies to attend the birth of her child. But she longed by day for the luxury of the night, when she could cry, and beg Thorpe under her breath to come to her.

When the next steamer arrived it brought her no letter from Thorpe. But this was to be expected. Another steamer arrived; it brought nothing. She turned very grey.

"Make a close calculation," she said to Miss Shropshire. "You know how long it takes to go to Cuba and back. Has there been time?"

"Yes, there has been time."

It was the middle of February, the end of a mild and beautiful winter. Little rain had fallen. Nature seemed to Nina more caressing than ever. The sun rarely veiled his face with a passing cloud. She worked with feverish persistence, keeping up her spirits as best she could. There was a bare chance that the next steamer would bring Thorpe.

Her father had paid her another visit, and gone away unsuspicious. He had, in fact, talked of nothing but the approaching rebellion of the Southern States, and the possible effect on the progress of the country. It was not likely that he would come again, for he had embarked on two new business enterprises, and he allowed himself to believe that Nina had passed the danger point.

The third steamer arrived. It brought neither Thorpe nor a letter. Then Nina gave way. For twenty-four hours she wept and sobbed, paying no attention to expostulations and threats. Miss Shropshire was seriously alarmed; for the first time she fully realised the proportions of the responsibility she had assumed. She longed for advice. She even contemplated sending for Mr. Randolph; for with all her dogged strength of character she was but a woman, and an unmarried one. Finally she wrote to Clough, who had arrived in Napa a fortnight before. She could not bring herself to betray Nina's confidence; but Clough already knew. Then she went to her room, and cursed Thorpe roundly and aloud. After that she felt calmer, and returned to Nina.

"I can't think he is dead," said Nina, abruptly, speaking coherently for the first time. "If he were, I should know it. I should *see* him." Miss Shropshire shivered, and cast an apprehensive glance into the dark corners of the room. "But he is ill; That is the only explanation. You don't doubt him?" turning fiercely to her friend.

"No; I can't say that I do. No —" with some reluctance, "decidedly not. He's not that sort. Like most men, he will probably cool off in time; but he's no weathercock, and one could hardly help believing in his honesty."

Nina kissed her with passionate gratitude. "I could n't stand having you doubt him," she said. "I never have, not for a moment; but — oh — what does it matter what is the reason? He has n't come, and I have n't heard from him. That is enough!"

"There will be one more steamer. There is just time."

"He won't come. I *feel* that everything is going wrong. One way and another, my life is going to ruin —"

"Nonsense, you are merely overwrought and despondent —"

"That is not all. And I know myself. Listen — if my baby dies, and he does not come, I shall go down lower than I have ever been, and I shall stay there. I 'd never rise again, nor want to —"

"Then, for Heaven's sake, don't do your best to kill it! Brace up. I believe that a good deal of what you say is true. Some people are strong for the pleasure of giving other people a chance to add to the platitudes of the world; but you are not that sort. So take care of yourself."

"Very well; put me to bed. I will do what I can."

She did not rise the next day, and, when Clough came, consented, listlessly, to see him. In this interview he made no impression on her whatever; he might have been an automaton. Her brain realised no man but the one for whom her weary heart ached.

She made an effort on the following day, and embroidered, and listened while Miss Shropshire read aloud to her. The effort was renewed daily; and every hour she fought with her instinct to succumb to despair. Physically, she was very tired. She longed for the care and tenderness which would have been hers in happier circumstances.

VI

Miss Shropshire took the precaution to ask Clough to come to the cottage a day or two before the next steamer was due, and to be prepared to remain. The steamer arrived, and with it nothing of interest to Nina Randolph.

She was very ill. Even Clough, who was inimitable in a sick room, looked grey and anxious. But it passed; and the time came when the housekeeper, who had had many babies in her time, placed a little girl in Nina's arms.

Nina, who had been lying with closed eyes, exhausted and wretched, turned her face toward the unfamiliar weight, and looked wonderingly into the face of the child. For a moment she hardly realised its significance, vivid as had been her imaginings. The baby's colour was fair and agreeable, and its large blue eyes moved slowly about with an expression of sober inquiry.

Nina glanced hastily outward. She was alone for the moment. Miss Shropshire had gone to her well-earned rest, and Dr. Clough was in the dining-room, attended by Mrs. Atkins. Nina drew the baby closer, and kissed it. For the moment she held Dudley Thorpe in her arms, — for she could not grasp their separateness, — and peace returned. Thorpe was ill, of course; but he was hardy and young, and would recover. The rapture of young motherhood possessed her. She kissed the baby many times, softly, fearing that it might break, then drew back and gazed at it with rapt adoration. Once she met its wise solemn eyes, and the first soul of Dudley Thorpe looked from their depths. She moved it with trembling care, and laid its head on her breast.

She gave no thought to the time when the world must know; the world no longer existed for her. Dudley Thorpe was her husband, and his child was in her arms, — an actual tangible beautiful certainty; all the rest that went to make up life was nebulæ.

It was a very good baby, and gave little trouble; consequently Nina was permitted to hold it most of the time. She felt no desire to rise from the bed, to take an active part in life again. She would have liked to remain there until Thorpe came and sat beside her. She spoke little, excepting to the child, and perhaps those hours, despite the great want, were the happiest of her life.

"What are some women made of?" demanded Miss Shropshire of Dr. Clough. "What is she going to do with that baby? That's what I want to know. It may be months before Dudley Thorpe gets here, and it certainly won't be long before Mr. Randolph comes up again. I don't believe she has given a thought to the consequences — and I have always thought her an unusually bright and level-headed woman."

"I see nothing to do but let matters take their course." He hesitated a moment, then gave Miss Shropshire a swift tentative glance, shifting his eyes hastily. "Would you — you believe in my disinterestedness, do you not, Miss Molly?"

"I do, indeed. You have been a real friend. I'm sure I don't know what I should have done without you."

"Then — if Mr. Thorpe does not return,

when she has become convinced that he does not mean to return, will you help me to make her understand that I am only too willing to marry her and adopt her child?"

Miss Shropshire stared, then shook her head. "You don't know Nina. It would be years before she got over her infatuation for Dudley Thorpe, if ever; and by that time everybody would know. Besides, I don't share your distrust of Thorpe. He is selfish, and is probably travelling beyond the reach of mails; but he is the soul of honour: no one could doubt that."

"He may be dead."

"We should have heard by this time; and it would not help you if he were. Most likely it would kill her."

"We don't die so easily."

"The thing to consider now is that baby. It's a dear little thing, and looks less like putty than most babies; I can actually see a resemblance to Thorpe. But, all the same, its presence is decidedly embarrassing."

The baby solved the problem. It died when it was ten days old. Even Miss Shropshire, who scorned the emotions, shuddered and burst into tears at the awful agony in Nina's eyes. Nina did not cry, nor did she speak. When the child was dressed for its coffin, the housekeeper brought it to the bedside. Nina raised herself on her elbow, and gave it a long devouring glance. It looked like marble rather than wax, and its likeness to Dudley Thorpe was startling. The contours of infancy had disappeared in its brief severe illness, and the strong bold outlines of the man who had called it into being were reproduced in little. The dark hair fell over its forehead in the same way, the mouth had the same arch.

Miss Shropshire entered the room, and Nina spoke for the first time since the baby had given its sharp cry of warning.

"Take it up into the forest, and bury it between the two pines where my hammock was." And then she turned her back and stared at the wall.

Shortly after, Mr. Randolph was informed that Nina had had a brief but severe attack of rheumatic fever, and he paid her a hurried visit. He wondered at the change in her, but did not suspect the truth.

"She is pining for Thorpe, I suppose," he said to Miss Shropshire. "I cannot understand his silence; and now God knows when we'll hear from him, unless he managed to get North before April 19th. Something has happened, I am afraid. Poor child, she was not born under a lucky star! Is she all right otherwise?"

"Yes, it looks as if she were cured. But when she goes to San Francisco, she had better stay with me for a time. I don't think her mother's society would be the best thing for her while she is so despondent."

"By all means. And that detestable Clough?"

"He is really a first-rate doctor, and has been devotion itself."

"Very well: I shall send him a handsome cheque. But if he has any matrimonial designs, let him look out. Don't imagine I am blind. A man does not neglect a fresh practice for cousinly affection. I cannot suppose for a moment that she would tolerate him, but when a woman is listless and despondent, and thinks that all her prospects of happiness are over, there's no telling what she will do; particularly if the besieger has the tenacity of a bull dog. I 'd rather see her in her coffin than married to Richard Clough."

Miss Shropshire was very anxious to return to San Francisco. She loved Nina Randolph; but she had immured herself in the cause of friendship long enough, and thought that her afflicted friend would be quite as well off where distractions were more abundant. When she suggested return, Nina acquiesced indifferently, and Mrs. Atkins packed the trunks with a hearty good-will. Dr. Clough brought a hack, at great expense, from Napa, and packed her into it as if she were a baby. As it drove off, she looked through the window up to the forest where her baby lay. She had not been strong enough to climb to the grave. She knew that she should never see it.

BOOK III

BOOK III

I

When Thorpe left New Orleans his plan was to return on the next steamer but one, then to go North to New York or Boston,—he had friends in both cities,—and amuse himself in new fields until he was permitted to return to California. He sought distraction, for although he was reasonably sure of Nina's power to conquer herself, and intended to marry her whether she did or not, separation and time deepened his passion for her, and he only found peace of mind in filling his hours to the brim. It is doubtful if he would have consented to remain the year out were it not that he wished to admire her as much as she longed to have him. Her pride and confidence in herself would invigorate the happiness of both.

He left orders in New Orleans to have his mail held over until his return. Harold was very ill on the voyage. Almost immediately upon landing in Havana his health began to mend, and he declared himself ready to kiss the soil, as he could not bestow a similar mark of favour on the climate. He announced his intention of sending for his affianced and spending the rest of his life in the West Indies. Thorpe did not take him too seriously, but seeing that there was no prospect of getting away for some time, and believing that Cuba would offer himself entertainment for several months, he sent to New Orleans for his mail, and wrote to Nina announcing his present plans. Whether the letters never left the Havana post-office, or whether the mail sack was lost overboard later, or ignored in the excitement at New Orleans, no one will ever know. Nor does it matter; they were never received, and that is all that concerns this tale. Thorpe and Harold started inland immediately, and finally determined to go to Jamaica and San Domingo before returning to Havana. He knew it was worse than folly to trust letters to the wretched inland post-offices, and he had told Nina in his letter of explanation not to expect another for some time. He should be in New Orleans on the first of May, and, meanwhile, he kept a diary for her future entertainment.

While exploring the mountain forests in the central part of Hayti, their guide was murdered, and they were two months finding their way to San Domingo. They were months of excitement, adventure, and more than one hair-breadth escape. Thorpe would have been in his element had it been possible to communicate with Nina, and could he have been sure of getting out of the West Indies before the rainy season began. They came unexpectedly upon San Domingo; and he learned that war had broken out in the United States during April. They made what haste they could to Havana, Harold as eager to return to civilisation as his brother; for vermin and land-crabs had tempered his enthusiasm, and he had acquired a violent dislike for the negro. At Havana, Thorpe found no letters awaiting him. He also learned from an American resident that postal communication had ceased between the North and South on May 31st. He wondered blankly at his stupidity in not going North while there was yet time, but like many others, he had heard so much talk of war that he had ceased to believe in its certainty. He could only hope that his letter had reached Nina, but knew that it was more than doubtful. The Southern ports were in a state of blockade. He and his brother ran it in a little boat rowed by themselves. In New Orleans he read the packet of letters from Nina, that awaited him.

II

The great change in Nina Randolph's appearance and manner induced no small amount of gossip in San Francisco. Women are quick to scent the sin that society loves best to discuss, and there were many that suspected the truth: her long retirement had prepared them for an interesting sequel. Nina guessed that she was dividing with the war the honours of attention in a small but law-making circle, but was quite indifferent. She rarely went down to the parlour when people called, but sat in her bed-room staring out at the bay; the Lester house was on the summit of Clay Street hill.

Her father was deeply anxious, full of gloomy forebodings. He believed Thorpe to be dead, and shook with horror when he thought of what the consequences might be.

"Would n't you like a change?" he asked her one day. "How would you like go to New York? Molly and Mrs. Lester could go with you."

Nina shook her head, colouring faintly.

"I see. You are afraid of missing Thorpe. I wish there were some way of finding out —"

She turned to him with eager eyes. "Would you go, papa, — to New Orleans? I have n't dared to ask it. Go and see what is the matter."

"My child, I could not get there. The ports are blockaded; if I attempted the folly of getting to New Orleans by land, I should probably be shot as a spy. It is for those reasons that he will have great difficulty in getting here, as he did not have the forethought to leave the South in time."

To this Nina made no reply, and as she would not talk to him, he left her.

That evening Miss Shropshire came into Nina's room, and spoke twice before she was answered. The room was dark.

"Look here, Nina!" she said peremptorily. "You 've got to brace up. People are talking. I know it!"

"Are they? What does it matter? I have no more use for them. I may as well tell you I have come to the conclusion that Dudley Thorpe ceased to care for me, and that is the reason of his silence. He has gone back to England."

"I don't believe it. You 're growing morbid. Women frequently do after that sort of experience. I remember Beatrix sat in one position for nearly a month, staring at the floor: would n't even brush her teeth. You have too much brains for that sort of thing."

"I believe it. I have made up my mind. He is in England. He wrote me once that if it were not that I had asked him not to leave the country, he would run over, he was so tired of America. He went, and stayed."

"Well, then, go out in the world and flirt as you used to. Don't let any man bowl you over like this; and, for Heaven's sake, don't mope any more!"

"I hate the thought of every man in San Francisco. When I knew them, I was an entirely different woman. I could n't adapt myself to them if I wanted to — which I don't."

"But there are always new ones —"

"Oh, don't! Have n't you imagination enough to guess what this last year has made of me? If I got as far as a ball-room I 'd stand up in the middle of the floor and shriek out that since I was there last my heart had lived and been broken, that I had lost a husband and buried a baby —"

"Then, for Heaven's sake, stay at home! But I think," with deep meaning, "that you had better try a change of some sort, Nina. If you don't want to risk going East, why not visit some of the Spanish people in Southern California?"

"I shall stay here."

It was during the next night that Nina left her bed suddenly, flung herself into a chair, and pressed her elbows hard upon her knees. She had barely slept for three nights. Her nerves were in a highly irritable state. If any one had entered she would not have been able to control her temper. Black depression possessed her; the irritability of her nerves alternated with the sensation of dropping through space; and her relaxed body cried for stimulant.

She twisted her hands together, her face convulsed. "Why should I fight?" she argued aloud. "In that, at least, I should find temporary oblivion. And what else have I left? Down deep, ever since I got his last letter, I have known that I should never see him again. It is my destiny: that is the beginning and the end of it. This is the second time I have wanted it since the baby died. I *beat* it out of me the first time. I hoped — hoped — and if he were here I should win. If I could be happy, and go away with him, it would not come again: I know — *I know*. He could have got me some word by this. He is not dead. There is only one other explanation. Men are all alike, they say. Why should I struggle? For what? What have I to live for? I am the most wretched woman on earth."

But she did struggle. The dawn found her sitting there still, her muscles almost rigid. Her love for Thorpe had undergone no change; it took the fight into its own hands. And it seemed to her that she could hear her soul beg for its rights; its voice rose above the persistent clamour of her body.

She went to bed and slept for a few hours; but when she awoke the desire in her nerves was madder than ever. Every part of her cried out for stimulant. She had no love for the taste of liquor; the demand came from her nerve-centres. But still she fought on, materialising the monster, fancying that she held it by the throat, that she cut its limbs off, its heart out; but it shook itself together with magnificent vitality, and laughed in her face.

Days passed. The clamour in her body strove to raise itself above the despairing cry in her soul. But still, mechanically, without hope, she lifted her ear to the higher cry, knowing that if she fell now she should never rise again in her earthly life, nor speak with Dudley Thorpe, should he, perhaps, return.

She invoked the image of her baby, the glory of the few days she had known it. But a bitter tide of resentment overwhelmed the memory of that brief exaltation. If she was to be saved, why had not the baby been spared? Those who shared her secret had attempted to console her by assuring her that its death was a mercy for all concerned. She had not answered them; but her grief was cut with contempt for their lack of vision. The baby might have cost her her social position, but it would have stood between her soul and perdition. It had been taken — by One who was supposed to know the needs of all His creatures. Therefore it was only reasonable to assume that He wished her to be destroyed.

She thought of nothing else, but cunningly pretended to be absorbed in her books.

There came a night when her nerves shrieked until her brain surged with the din of them, and her hands clutched at the air, her eyes hardened and expanded with greed, her lips were forced apart by her panting breath. She jerked the stopper out of a bottle of cologne and swallowed a quarter of the contents, then flung her wraps about her, stole downstairs and out of the house, found a carriage, and was driven to South Park.

III

Two weeks later she sat huddled over the fire in the library. Her face was yellow; her eyes were sunken and dull; her hands trembled. She looked thirty-five.

In her lap lay a letter from Dudley Thorpe. He and his brother, at the risk of their lives, had got through the lines and reached New York. The excitement, fatigue, and exposure had nearly killed Harold, who was in a hospital in a precarious condition. Thorpe could not leave him. He implored her to come on to New York at once; and he had never written a more tender and passionate letter.

Cochrane opened the door, and announced that Dr. Clough had called.

"Tell him to come here," she said.

Dr. Clough wore his usual jaunty air, and he made no comment on her appearance; he had come straight from Miss Shropshire.

"Sit down," said Nina, curtly, interrupting his demonstrations. "You come at the right moment. I was about to send for you."

"My dear cousin Nina! I hope there is no —"

"Let me talk, please. Do you wish to marry me?"

Clough caught his breath. He flushed, despite his nerve. "Of course I do," he stammered. "What a question! Certainly there never was a woman so original. It is like you to settle matters in your own way."

"Don't delude yourself for a moment that I even like you. Of all the men I have ever known, the sort of person I take you to be has my most unmitigated contempt. It is for that reason I marry you. I must marry some one at once to keep myself from ruining the life of Dudley Thorpe. I choose you, because, in the first place, I am so vile a thing that no punishment is severe enough for me; and, in the second, Fate has acquitted herself so brilliantly in regard to my humble self that I feel a certain satisfaction in giving her all she wants."

"My dear Nina, you are morbid." He spoke pleasantly, but he turned away his eyes.

"Possibly; it would be somewhat remarkable if I were not. Do you still wish to marry me?"

"Certainly. I do not take your rather uncomplimentary utterances seriously. In your present frame of mind —"

"It is the only frame of mind I shall ever be in. You will have an unpleasant domestic life; but you will have all the money you want. Don't flatter yourself for a moment that you will either control or cure me. You will be no more in my house than a well-paid butler — after my father has been induced to accept you, which will not be in a hurry. Meanwhile, you will probably beat me: you are quite capable of it; but you may save yourself the exertion."

"I shall not beat you, Nina, dear." He

spoke softly, with an assumption of masculine indulgence; but his small pointed teeth moved suddenly apart.

"You will understand, of course, that this engagement must not get to my father's ears. He would lock me up before he would permit me to marry you. He has all the contempt of the gentleman for the cad, of the real man for the bundle of petty imitations: and you are his pet aversion. On the tenth, he is obliged to go to San José to attend an important law-suit. He will be detained not less than three days. We shall marry on the eleventh — at Mrs. Lester's. I shall not tell my mother, for I will not give her the pleasure of conspiring against my father. I suppose that I shall break my father's heart; but I don't know that I care. He might have saved me, if he had been stronger, and I am no longer capable of loving any one — "

"Suppose Mr. Thorpe should come out here after you, anyhow, married or not."

"He will do nothing of the sort. One reason you would be incapable of understanding, should I attempt to explain; the other is, that he will no longer want me after

I have been the wife of a person of your sort."

"My word, Nina, you are rather rough on a fellow; but give me a kiss, and I'll overlook it."

She lifted her face, and let him kiss her, then struck him so violent a blow that the little man staggered.

"Now go," she said, "and don't let me see you again until the eleventh. If you have anything to say, you can write it to Molly Shropshire."

When he had gone, she drew her hand across her lips, then looked closely at it as if expecting to see a stain. Then she shuddered, and huddled closer to the fire, and in a few moments threw Dudley Thorpe's letter on the coals.

IV

"Well, some women *are* remarkable!" exclaimed Miss Shropshire to her sister, Mrs. Lester. "The idea of her having a wedding dress,—white satin, train, and all.

She even fussed over at least twenty pairs of slippers, and I was almost afraid to bring home that bridal veil for fear it would n't suit her."

"I suppose she thinks that weddings, white satin ones, at least, only come once in a lifetime." Mrs. Lester was a tired little woman, quite subservient to her strong-minded sister. The wedding was to take place in her back parlour at an hour when Mr. Lester, occupied and unsuspecting, would be away from home. She did not approve of the plot; but her opinion, much less her consent, had not been asked.

"I'd like to thoroughly understand Nina Randolph, just for once," said Miss Shropshire, meditatively. "It would be interesting, to say the least."

The night before the wedding she went into Nina's room, and found her standing before the mirror arrayed in her bridal finery, — veil, gloves, slippers, all. She had regained her natural hues; but her eyes were still sunken, her face pinched and hard. She was almost plain.

"Nina! Why on earth have you put on

those things? Don't you know it's bad luck?"

Nina laughed.

Miss Shropshire exclaimed, "*Umburufen!*" and rapped loudly three times on the top of a chair. "There! I hope that will do some good. I know what you are thinking — you are so unlucky, anyhow. But why tempt fate?" She hesitated a moment. "It is not too late. Put it off for six months, and then see how you feel about it. You are morbid now. You don't know what changes time might —"

"No earthly power can prevent me from marrying Richard Clough to-morrow."

"Very well, I shall stand by you, of course. That goes without saying. But I believe you are making a terrible mistake. I would rather you married almost any one else. There are several gentlemen that would be ready and willing."

"I don't wish to marry a gentleman."

The next afternoon Nina, Mrs. Lester, and Miss Shropshire were in the back parlour awaiting the arrival of Clough, his best man, and the clergyman, when there was a sudden furious pull at the bell of the front door. Nina sprang to her feet. For the first time in many weeks animation sprang to her eyes.

"It is my father!" she said. "Close the folding-doors. Molly, I rely on you! Do you understand? Send him away, and as quickly as possible. Tell a servant to watch outside, and take the others round the back way."

Before she had finished speaking, Mr. Randolph's voice was heard in the hall, demanding his daughter. The servants had been given orders to deny the fact of Miss Randolph's presence in the house to any one but Dr. Clough. Nevertheless, Mr. Randolph brushed past the woman that opened the door, and entered the front parlour. Miss Shropshire joined him at once. Every word of the duologue that followed could be heard on the other side of the folding-doors.

"Why, Mr. Randolph!" exclaimed Miss Shropshire, easily. "Why this unexpected honour? I thought you were in San José."

"Is my daughter here?" He was evidently much excited, and endeavouring to control himself.

"Nina? No. Why? Is she not at Redwoods? She was to go down yesterday."

"She is not at Redwoods. I have received private and reliable information that she is to marry Richard Clough this afternoon, and I have reason to think that she is in this house."

"What? Nina going to marry that horrid little man? I don't believe it!" Miss Shropshire was a woman of thorough and uncompromising methods.

"Is Nina in this house or not?"

"Mr. Randolph! Of course she is not. I would have nothing to do with such an affair."

Mr. Randolph swallowed a curse, and strode up and down the room several times. Then he paused and confronted her once more.

"Molly," he said, "I appeal to you as a woman. If you have any friendship for Nina, give her up to me and save her from ruin, or tell me where she is. It is not yet too late. I will risk everything and take her abroad. She is ruining her own life and Thorpe's and mine by a mistaken sense of duty to him, and contempt for herself: I know her so well that I feel sure that is the reason for this act she contemplates to-day. I will take her to Thorpe. He could reclaim her. Clough — you can perhaps imagine how Clough will treat her! Picture the life she must lead with that man, and give her up to me. And, if you have any heart, keep my own from breaking. She is all that I have. You know what my home is; I have lived in hell for twenty-four years for this girl's sake. I have kept a monster in my house that Nina should have no family scandal to reproach me with. And all to what purpose if she marries a cad and a brute? I would have endured the torments of the past twenty-five years, multiplied tenfold, to have secured her happiness. If she marries Richard Clough, it will kill me."

"She is not here," replied Miss Shropshire.

Mr. Randolph trembled from head to foot. "My God!" he cried, "have you women no heart? Are all women, I wonder, like those I have known? My wife, a demon who nursed her baby on brandy! My daughter, repaying the devotion of years with blackest ingratitude! And you —" He fell, rather than dropped to his knees, and caught her dress in his hands.

"Molly," he prayed, "give her to me. Save her from becoming one of the outcast of the earth. For that is what this marriage will mean to her."

Miss Shropshire set her teeth. "Nina is not here," she said.

Mr. Randolph stumbled to his feet, and rushed from the house. He walked rapidly down the hill toward Old Trinity in Pine Street, the church Nina attended, his dislocated mind endeavouring to suggest that he wait for her there. His agitation was so marked that several people turned and looked after him in surprise. He reached the church. A carriage approached, passed. Its occupants were Richard Clough, a well-known gambler named Bell, and a man who carried the unmistakable cut of a parson.

Mr. Randolph rushed to the middle of the street, ordering the driver to stop. The window of the carriage was open. He caught Clough by the shoulder.

"Are you on your way to marry my daughter?" he demanded.

"My dear Uncle James," replied the young man, airily, "you are all wrong. I am on my way to marry — it is true; but the unfortunate lady is Miss McCullum."

Mr. Randolph turned to the gambler, and implored him, as a man of honour, to tell him the truth.

Bell replied: "As a man of honour, I dare not."

Mr. Randolph appealed to the clergyman, but met only a solemn scowl, and mechanically dropped back, with the sensation of having lost the good-will of all men. A moment later the carriage was rattling up the street at double speed, and he cursed his stupidity in not forcing an entrance, or hanging on behind. There was no other carriage in sight.

V

THE days were very long to Dudley Thorpe. The invalid recovered slowly, and demanded much of his time. Before an answer to his letter could be expected, Harold was sufficiently mended to be removed to the house of a friend on Long Island. He declared his intention of sailing for California as soon as he could obtain the doctor's permission to travel. The lady to whom he was betrothed came over from England and married him; and Thorpe had little to do but to think.

He bitterly reproached himself that he had asked Nina to come to New York, instead of trusting to his brother's recuperative powers, and starting at once for California. He dared not go now, lest he pass her. But he was beset by doubts, and some of them were nightmares. She would come if her child had lived, and she had weathered her year. If she had not! He knew what she had suffered during that year, would have guessed without the aid of the few letters she had written after letters from him had ceased to reach California. Exposure and shame might have come to her since. If he could have been sure that she believed in him, he would have feared little; but it was not to be expected that she had received a letter he had sent her from the West Indies. The telegraph has averted many a tragedy, but there was none across the United States. With all his will and health and wealth and love, he had been as powerless to help her in the time of her great trouble, was as powerless to help her now, as if he were in the bottom of a Haytian swamp. All that was fine in him, and there was much, was thoroughly roused. He not only longed for her and for his child, but he vowed to devote the rest of his life to her happiness. It seemed to him incredible that he could have committed such a series of mistakes; that no man who loved a woman with the passion of his life had ever so consistently done the wrong thing. But mistakes are not isolated acts, to be plucked out of life and viewed as an art student views his first model, in which he finds only a few bald lines; even when the pressure of many details is not overwhelming it often clouds the mental vision. Years after, Thorpe accepted the fact that the great links in that year's chain of events were connected by hundreds of tiny links as true of form; but not then.

One day a budget of mail got through the lines, and in it was a letter for him. It was from Nina, and was dated shortly after the last he had found awaiting him when he arrived from Cuba.

> I don't know where you are, if you will ever get this; but I must write to you. The baby is dead. It was a little girl. It is buried in the forest.
>
> NINA.

The steamer by which he expected her arrived a few days later. It brought him the following letter:

> I was married yesterday. My name is Mrs. Richard Clough. My husband is the son of a Haworth cobbler. I received your letter.
>
> NINA RANDOLPH CLOUGH.

VI

Mr. and Mrs. Harold Thorpe sailed on the next steamer for California. Dudley Thorpe worked his way South, offered his services to the Confederacy, fought bitterly and brilliantly, when he was not in hospital with a bullet in him, rose to the rank of colonel, and made a name for himself which travelled to California and to England. At the close of the war, he returned home and entered Parliament. He became known as a hard worker, a member of almost bitter honesty, and a forcible and magnetic speaker. Socially he was, first, a lion, afterward, a steady favourite. Altogether he was regarded as a success by his fellow-men.

It was some years before he heard from his brother. Harold was delighted with the infinite variety of California; his health was remarkably good; and he had settled for life. Only his first letter contained a reference to Nina Randolph. She had lived in Napa for a time, then gone to Redwoods. She never came to San Francisco; therefore he had been unable to call, had never even seen her. All Thorpe's other friends had been very kind to himself and his wife.

Thorpe long before this had understood. The rage and disgust of the first months had worn themselves out, given place to his intimate knowledge of her. Had he returned to California it would have been too late to do her any good, and would have destroyed the dear memory of her he now possessed. He still loved her. For many months the pain of it had been unbearable. It was unbearable no longer, but he doubted if he should ever love another woman. The very soul of him had gone out to her, and if it had returned he was not conscious of it. As the years passed, there were long stretches when she did not enter his thought, when memory folded itself thickly about her and slept. Time deals kindly with the wounds of men. And he was a man of active life, keenly interested in the welfare of his country. But he married no other woman.

It was something under ten years since he had left California, when he received a letter from his sister-in-law stating that his brother was dead, and begging him to come out and settle her affairs, and take her home. She had neither father nor brother; and he went at once, although he had no desire to see California again.

There were rails between New York and San Francisco by this time, and he found the latter a large flourishing and hideous city. The changes were so great, the few acquaintances he met during the first days of his visit looked so much older, that his experience of ten years before became suddenly blurred of outline. He was not quite forty; but he felt like an old man groping in his memory for an episode of early youth. The eidolon of Nina Randolph haunted him, but with ever-evading lineaments. He did not know whether to feel thankful or disappointed.

He devoted himself to his sister-in-law's affairs for a week, then, finding a Sunday afternoon on his hands, started, almost reluctantly, to call on Mrs. McLane.

South Park was unchanged.

He stood for a moment, catching his breath. The city had grown around and away from it; streets had multiplied, bristling with the ugliest varieties of modern architecture; but South Park, stately, dark, solemn, had not changed by so much as a lighter coat of paint. His eyes moved swiftly to the Randolph house. Its shutters were closed. The dust of summer was thick upon them. He stood for fully five minutes staring at it, regardless of curious eyes. Something awoke and hungered within him.

"My vanished youth, I suppose," he thought sadly. "I certainly have no wish to see her, poor thing! But she was very sweet."

He walked slowly round the crescent on the left, and rang the bell at Mrs. McLane's door. As the butler admitted him he noted with relief that the house had been refurnished. A buzz of voices came from the parlour. The man lifted a portière, and Mrs. McLane, with an exclamation of delight, came forward, with both hands outstretched. Her face was unchanged, but she would powder her hair no more. It was white.

"Thorpe!" she exclaimed. "It is not possible? How long have you been here?

A week! Mon Dieu! And you come only now! But I suppose I am fortunate to be remembered at all."

Thorpe assured her that she had been in his thoughts since the hour of his arrival, but that he wished to be free of the ugly worries of business before venturing into her distracting presence.

"I don't forgive you, although I give you a dinner on Thursday. Will that suit you? Poor little Mrs. Harold! We have all been attention itself to her for your sake. Come here and sit by me; but you may speak to your other old friends."

Two of the "Macs" were there; the other was dead, he was told later. Both were married, and one was dressed with the splendours of Paris. Mrs. Earle was as little changed as Mrs. McLane, and her still flashing eyes challenged him at once. Guadalupe Hathaway was unmarried and had grown stout; but she was as handsome as of old.

They all received him with flattering warmth, "treated him much better than he deserved," Mrs. McLane remarked, "considering he had never written one of them a line;" and he felt the past growing sharp of outline. There were several very smart young ladies present, two of whom he remembered as awkward little girls. The very names of the others were unknown to him. They knew of him, however, and one of them affected to disapprove of him sharply because he had "fought against the flag." Mrs. McLane took up the cudgels for her South, and party feeling ran high.

Nina Randolph's name was not mentioned. He wondered if she were dead. Not so much as a glance was directed toward the most momentous episode of his life. Doubtless they had forgotten that he had once been somewhat attentive to her. But his memory was breaking in the middle and marshalling its forces at the farther end; the events of the intervening ten years were now a confused mass of shadows. Mrs. Earle sang a Mexican love-song, and he turned the leaves for her. When he told Guadalupe Hathaway that he was glad to find her unchanged, she replied: —

"I am fat, and you know it. And as I don't mind in the least, you need not fib about it. You have a few grey hairs and lines; but you 've worn better than our men, who are burnt out with trade winds and money grubbing."

He remained an hour. When he left the house, he walked rapidly out of the Park, casting but one hasty glance to the right, crossed the city and went straight to the house of Molly Shropshire's sister. It also was unchanged, a square ugly brown house on a corner over-looking the blue bay and the wild bright hills beyond. The houses that had sprung up about it were cheap and fresh, and bulging with bow-windows.

"Yes," the maid told him, "Miss Shropshire still lived there, and was at home." The room into which she showed him was dark, and had the musty smell of the unpopular front parlour. A white marble slab on the centre table gleamed with funereal significance. Thorpe drew up the blinds, and let in the sun. He was unable to decide if the room had been refurnished since the one occasion upon which he had entered it before; but it had an old-fashioned and dingy appearance.

He heard a woman's gown rustle down the stair, and his nerves shook. When Miss Shropshire entered, she did not detect his effort at composure. She had accepted the flesh of time, and her hair was beginning to turn; but she shook hands in her old hearty decided fashion.

"I heard yesterday that you were here," she said. "Take that armchair. I rather hoped you 'd come. We used to quarrel; but, after all, you are an Englishman, and I can never forget that I was born over there, although I don't remember so much as the climate."

"Will you tell me the whole story? I did not intend to come to see you, to mention her name. But it has come back, and I must know all that there is to know — from the very date of my leaving up to now. Of course, she wrote me that you were in her confidence."

She told the story of a year which had been as big with import for one woman as for a nation. "Mr. Randolph died six months after the wedding," she concluded, wondering if some men were made of stone. "It killed him. He did not see her again until he was on his death-bed. Then he forgave her. Any one would, poor thing. He left his money in trust, so that she has a large income, and is in no danger of losing it. She lives with her mother at Redwoods. Clough died some years ago — of drink. It was in his blood, I suppose, for almost from the day he set foot in Redwoods he was a sot."

"And Nina?"

"Don't try to see her," said Miss Shropshire, bluntly. "You would only be horrified, — you would n't recognise her if you met her on the street. She is breaking, fortunately. I saw her the other day, for the first time in two years, and she told me she was very ill."

"Have you deserted her?"

"Don't put it that way! I shall always love Nina Randolph, and I am often sick with pity. But she never comes here, and one *cannot* go to Redwoods. It is said that the orgies there beggar description. Even the Hathaways, who are their nearest neighbours, never enter the gates. It is terrible! And if your letter had come six days earlier, it would all have been different. But she was born to bad luck."

Thorpe rose. "Thank you," he said. "Are your sisters well? I shall be here only a few days longer, but I shall try to call again."

She laid her hand on his arm. She had a sudden access of vision. "Don't try to see Nina," she said, impressively.

"God forbid!" he said.

VII

He slept not at all that night. He had thought that his days of poignant emotion were over, that he had worn out the last of it on the blood-soaked fields of Virginia, on nights between days when Death rose with the sun; but up from their long sleep misery and love rose with the vigour of their youth, and claimed him. And the love was for a woman who no longer existed, whose sodden brain doubtless held no memory of him, or remembered only to curse him. He strove to imagine her as she must be. She rose before him in successive images of what she had been: from the night he had met her to the morning of their last interview on the mountain,—a series of images sometimes painful, always beautiful. Then his imagination created her as she must have been during the months of her solitude in the midst of a wild and beautiful country, when in her letters she had sent him so generous and so exquisite a measure of herself; then the last months, when he would have been half mad with love and pity if he had known. Nor was that all: it seemed to him in the torments of that night that he realised for the first time what he had lost, what poignant, enduring, and varied happiness might have been his during the past ten years. Instead, he had had excitement, honours, and mental activity; he had not been happy for an hour. And the possibility of such happiness, of union with the one woman whom he was capable of passionately loving with soul and mind and body, was as dead as his youth, buried with the soul of a woman whose face he would not recognise. She was above ground, this woman, and a different being! He repeated the fact aloud; but it was the one fact his imagination would not grasp and present to his mental vision. It realised her suffering, her morbid despair, her attitude to herself, to the world, and to him, when she had decided to marry Clough; but the hideous metamorphosis of body and spirit was outside its limitations.

In the morning he asked his sister-in-law if she would leave California at the end of the week. She was a methodical and slow-moving little person, and demurred for a time, but finally consented to make ready. Her business affairs — which consisted of several unsold ranches — could be left in the hands of an agent; there was little more that her brother-in-law could do.

Harold's remains had been temporarily placed in the receiving vault on Lone Mountain. Thorpe went out to the cemetery in the afternoon to make the final arrangements for removing them to England.

Lone Mountain can be seen from any part of San Francisco; scarcely a house but has a window from which one may receive his daily hint that even Californians are mortal. Here is none of the illusion of the cemetery of the flat, with its thickly planted trees and shrubbery, where the children are taken to walk when they are good, and to wonder at the glimpses of pretty little white houses and big white slates with black letters. The shining tombs and vaults and monuments, tier above tier, towering at the end of the city, flaunt in one's face the remorselessness and the greed of death. In winter, the paths are running brooks; one imagines that the very dead are soaked. In summer, the dusty trees and shrubs accentuate the marble pride of dead and living men. Behind, higher still, rises a bare brown mountain with a cross on its summit, — Calvary it is called; and on stormy nights, or on days when the fog is writhing in from the ocean, blurring even that high sharp peak, one fancies the trembling outlines of a figure on the cross.

To-day the tombs were scarcely visible within the fine white mist which had been creeping in from the Pacific since morning and had made a beautiful ghost-land of the entire city. The cross on Calvary looked huge and misshapen, the marbles like the phantoms of those below. The mist dripped heavily from the trees, the walks were wet. It is doubtful if there is so gloomy, so disturbing, so fascinating a burying-ground on earth as the Lone Mountain of San Francisco.

The sexton's house was near the gates. Thorpe completed his business, and started for the carriage which had brought him. He paused for a moment in the middle of the broad road and looked up. In the gently moving mist the shafts seemed to leave their dead, and crawl through the groves, as if to some ghoulish tryst. Thorpe thought that it would be a good place for a man, if lost, to go mad in. But, like all the curious phases of California, it interested him, and in a moment he sauntered slowly upward. His own mood was not hilarious, and although he had no wish to join the cold hearts about him, he liked their company for the moment.

Some one approached him from above. It was a woman, and she picked her way carefully down the steep hill-side. She loomed oddly through the mist, her outlines shifting.

As she passed Thorpe, he gave her the cursory glance of man to unbeautiful woman. She was short and stout; her face was dark and large, her hair grizzled about the temples, her expression sullen and dejected, her attire rich. She lifted her eyes, and stopped short.

"Dudley!" she said; and Thorpe recognised her voice.

He made no attempt to answer her. He was hardly conscious of anything but the wish that he had left California that morning.

"You did not recognise me?" she said, with a laugh he did not remember.

"No."

He stared at her, trying to conjure up the woman who had haunted him during the night. She had gone. There was a dim flash in the eyes, a broken echo in the voice of this woman, which gave him the impression of looking upon the faded daguerreotype of one long dead, or upon a bundle of old letters.

Her face dropped under his gaze. "I had hoped never to see you again," she muttered.

"But I don't know that I care much. It is long since I have thought of you. I care for one thing only, — nothing else matters. Still, I have a flicker of pride left: I would rather you should not have seen me an ugly old sot. I believe I was very pretty once; but I have forgotten."

Thorpe strove to speak, to say something to comfort the poor creature in her mortification; but he could only stare dumbly at her, while something strove to reach out of himself into that hideous tomb and clasp the stupefied soul which was no less his than in the brief day when they had been happy together. As long as that body lived on, it carried his other part. And after? He wondered if he could feel more alone then than now, did it take incalculable years for his soul to find hers.

She looked up and regarded him sullenly. "You are unchanged," she said. "Life has prospered with you, I suppose. I have n't read the papers nor heard your name mentioned for years; but I read all I could find about you during the war; and you look as if you had had few cares. Are you married?"

"No."

"You have been true to me, I suppose." And again she laughed.

"Yes, I suppose that is the reason. At least I have cared to marry no other woman."

"Hm!" she said. "Well, the best thing you can do is to forget me. I'm sorry if I hurt your pride, but I don't feel even flattered by your constancy. I have neither heart nor vanity left; I am nothing but an appetite,—an appetite that means a long sight more to me than you ever did. To-morrow, I shall have forgotten your existence again. Once or twice a year, when I am sober,—comparatively,—I come here to visit my father's tomb. Why, I can hardly say, unless it is that I find a certain satisfaction in contemplating my own niche. I am an unconscionable time dying."

"Are you dying?"

"I'm gone to pieces in every part of me. My mother threw me downstairs the other day, and that did n't mend matters."

"Come," he said. "I have no desire to prolong this interview. There is a private carriage at the gate. Is it yours? Then, if you will permit me, I will see you to it."

She walked beside him without speaking again. He helped her into her carriage, lifted his hat without raising his eyes, then dismissed his carriage, and walked the miles between the burying-ground and his hotel.

VIII

FOUR days later he received a note from Miss Hathaway: —

"Nina Randolph is dying; I have just seen her doctor, who is also ours. I do not know if this will interest you. She is at Redwoods."

An hour later Thorpe was in the train. He had not stopped to deliberate. Nothing could alter the fact that Nina Randolph was his, and eternally. He responded to the summons as instinctively as if she had been his wife for the past ten years. Nor did he shrink from the death-bed scene; hell itself could not be worse than the condition of his mind had been during the past four days.

There was no trap for hire at the station; he walked the mile to the house. It was a pale-blue blazing day. The May sun shone with the intolerable Californian glare. The roads were already dusty. But when he reached the avenue at Redwoods, the temperature changed at once. The trees grew close together, and the creek, full to the top, cooled the air; it was racing merrily along, several fine salmon on its surface. He experienced a momentary desire to spear them. Suddenly he returned to the gates; he had carried into the avenue a sense of something changed. He looked down the road sharply, — the road up which he had come the last time he had visited Redwoods, choking on a lumbering stage. Then he looked up the wooded valley, and back again. It was some moments before he realised wherein lay the change that had disturbed his introspective vision;

one of the great redwoods that had stood by the bridge where the creek curved just beyond the entrance to the grounds, was gone. He wondered what had happened to it, and retraced his steps.

The house, the pretty little toy castle with its yellow-plastered brown-trimmed walls, looked the same; he had but an indistinct memory of it. Involuntarily, his gaze travelled to the mountains; they were a mass of blurred redwoods in a dark-blue mist. But they were serene and beautiful; so was all nature about him.

He rang the bell. Cochrane opened the door. The man had aged; but his face was as stolid as ever.

"Mr. Thorpe, sir?" he said.

"Yes; I wish to see Miss — Mrs. Clough."

"She won't live the day out, sir."

"Show me up to her room. I shall stay here. Is any one else with her?"

"No, sir; Mrs. Randolph has been no good these two days, and the maid that has been looking out for Miss Nina is asleep. I 've been giving her her medicine. We don't like strange nurses here. Times are changed, and everybody knows now; but we keep to ourselves as much as possible. There 've been times when we 've had company — too much; but I made up my mind they should die alone. You can go up, though."

"Thanks. You can go to sleep, if you wish."

Cochrane led him down the hall with its beautiful inlaid floor, scratched and dull, up the wide stair with its faded velvet carpet, and opened the door of a large front room.

"The drops on the table are to be given every hour, sir; the next at twenty minutes to two." He closed the door and went away.

The curtains of the room were wide apart. The sun flaunted itself upon the old carpet, the handsome old-fashioned furniture. Thorpe went straight to the windows, and drew the curtains together, then walked slowly to the bed.

Nina lay with her eyes open, watching him intently. Her face was pallid and sunken; but she looked less unlike her old self. She took his hand and pressed it feebly.

"I am sorry I spoke so roughly the other day," she said. "But I was not quite myself. I have touched nothing since; I could n't, after seeing you. It is that that is killing me; but don't let it worry you. I am very glad."

Thorpe sat down beside her and chafed her hands gently. They were cold.

"It was a beautiful little baby," she said, abruptly. "And it looked so much like you that it was almost ridiculous."

"I was a brute to have left you, whether you wished it or not. It is no excuse to say that the consequences never entered my head, I was half mad that morning; and after what you had told me, I think I was glad to get away for a time."

"We both did what we believed to be best, and ruined — well, my life, and your best chance of happiness, perhaps. It is often so, I notice. Too much happiness is not a good thing for the world, I suppose. It is only the people of moderate desires and capacities that seem to get what they want. But it was a great pity; we could have been very happy. Did you care much?"

He showed her his own soul then, naked and tormented, — as it had been from the hour he had received her letters upon his return from the West Indies until Time had done its work upon him,—and as it was now and must be for long months to come. Of the intervening years he gave no account; he had forgotten them. She listened with her head eagerly lifted, her vision piercing his. He made the story short. When he had finished, her head fell back. She gave a long sigh. Was it of content? She made no other comment. She was past conventions; her emotions were already dead. And she was at last in that stage of development wherein one accepts the facts of life with little or no personal application.

"It did n't surprise me when you came in," she said, after a moment. "I felt that you would come— My life has been terrible, terrible! Do you realise that! Have they told you? No woman has ever fallen lower than I have done. I am sorry, for your sake; I can't repent in the ordinary way. I have an account to square with God, if I ever meet Him and He presumes to judge me. If you will forgive me, that is all that I care about."

"I forgive you! Good God, I wonder you don't hate me!"

"I did for a time, not because I blamed you, but because I hated everybody and everything. There were intervals of terrible retrospect and regret; but I made them as infrequent as I could, and finally I stifled them altogether. I grew out of touch with every memory of a life when I was comparatively innocent and happy. I strove to make myself so evil that I could not distinguish an echo if one tried to make itself heard; and I succeeded. Now, all that has fallen from me,—in the last few hours, since I have had relief from physical torments,—for I could not drink after I saw you, and I had to pay the penalty. It is not odd, I suppose, that I should suddenly revert: my impulses originally were all toward good, my mental impulses; the appetite was always a purely physical thing; and when Death approaches, he stretches out a long hand and brushes aside the rubbish of life, letting the soul's flower see the light again for a few moments. Give me the drops. Now that you are here, I want to live as long as I can."

He lifted her head, and gave her the medicine. She lay back suddenly, pinioning his arm.

"Let it stay there," she said.

"Are you sure, Nina, that your case is so bad?" he asked. "Could n't you make an effort, and let me take you to England?"

She shook her head with a cynical smile. "My machinery is like a dilapidated old engine that has been eaten up with rust, and battered by stones for twenty years. There is n't a bit of me that is n't in pieces."

She closed her eyes, and slept for a half hour. He put both arms about her and his head beside hers.

"Dudley," she said, finally.

"Well?"

"I had not thought of the baby for God knows how many years. It was no memory for me. But since the other day I have been haunted by that poor little grave in the big forest — "

"Would you like to have it brought down to Lone Mountain?"

She hesitated a moment, then shook her head.

"No," she said. "In the vault with my mother and — and — *him?* Oh, no! no!"

"If I build a little vault for you and her will you sign a paper giving me — certain rights?"

Her face illuminated for the first time. "Oh, yes!" she said. "Oh, yes! Then I think I could sleep in peace."

Thorpe rang for Cochrane and the gardener, wrote the paper, and had it duly witnessed. It took but a few moments, and they were alone again.

"I wonder if I shall see *her* — and you again, or if my unlucky star sets in this world to rise in the next? Well, I shall know soon.

"I am going, I think," she said a few moments later. "Would you mind kissing me? Death has already taken the sin out of my body, and down deep is something that never was wholly blackened. That is yours. Take it."

It was an hour before she died, and during that hour he kissed her many times.

A FRAGMENT

It was some twelve years later that Thorpe received a copy of a San Francisco newspaper, in which the following article was heavily marked:—

WHAT AM I BID?

AN AUCTION SALE OF FUNERAL AND WEDDING TRAPPINGS

"What am I offered?"

"Oh, don't sell that!" said one or two bidders.

The auctioneer held up a large walnut case. It contained a funeral wreath of preserved flowers.

"Well, I've sold coffins at auction in my time, so I guess I can stand this," replied the auctioneer. "What am I offered?"

He disposed of it, with three other funeral mementos, very cheap, for the bidding was dispirited. It was at the sale yesterday, in a Montgomery Street auction-room, of the personal effects, jewelry, silverware, and household bric-a-brac of a once very wealthy San Francisco family. The head of the family was a pioneer, a citizen of wealth and high social and commercial standing. It was he who, in early days, projected South Park. There was no family in the city whose society was more sought after, or which entertained better, than that of James Randolph.

"What am I offered for this lot?"

He referred to the lot catalogued as "No. 107," and described as "Wedding-dress, shoes, etc."

"Don't sell *that!*" The very old-clo' man remonstrated this time.

It seemed worse than the sale of the funeral wreath. The dress was heavy white satin — had been, that is; it was yellowed with time. The tiny shoes had evidently been worn but once.

"What am I offered? Make a bid, gentlemen. I offer the lot. What am I offered?"

"One dollar."

"One dollar I am offered for the lot — wedding-dress, shoes, etc. One dollar for the lot. Come gentlemen, bid up."

Not an old-clo' man in the room bid, and the outsider who bid the dollar had the happiness to see it knocked down to him.

"What am I bid for this photograph album? Bid up, gentlemen. Here's a chance to get a fine collection of photographs of distinguished citizens, their wives, and daughters."

A gentleman standing on the edge of the crowd quietly bid in the album. When it was handed to him, he opened it, took out his own and the photographs of several ladies, dressed in the fashion of twenty years ago, and tossed the album, with the other photographs, in the stove, remarking: "Well, *they* won't go to the junk-shop."

"What am I offered, gentlemen, for this? There is just seventeen dollars' worth of gold in it. Bid up."

The auctioneer held up an engraved gold medal. It was a Crimean war medal which its owner was once proud to wear. There was a time in his life when no money could have purchased it. He had risked his life for the honour of wearing it; and after his death it was offered for old gold.

"Twenty dollars."

"Twenty dollars; twenty, twenty, twenty! Mind your bid, gentlemen. Seventeen dollars for the gold, and three for the honour. Twenty, tw-en-ty, and going, going, gone! Seventeen dollars for the gold, and three for the honour."

In this way an ebony writing-desk, with the dead citizen's private letters, was sold to a hand-me-down shop-keeper. A tin box with private papers went to a junk-dealer; and different lots of classical music, some worn, some marked with the givers' names, some with verses written on the pages, were sold to second-hand dealers. "What am I bid?" The sale went rapidly on. Sometimes an old family friend would bid in an article as a souvenir. But the junk-dealers, second-hand men, and hand-me-down shop-keepers took in most of the goods.

The above articles were the contents of a chest, and were the personal effects of Mrs. Richard Clough, the late daughter of the late James Randolph, of San Francisco. She had evidently carefully packed them away at some time before her death; and the chest had been mislaid or overlooked, until it made its way, intact, and twelve years after, into the hands of the public.

And that was the last that Dudley Thorpe heard of Nina Randolph in this world.

THE END